Rooke, Rasheem
Black Ribisi
Roxbury Warburton Publishing

Dedicated to "*Crow*" and "*Taffy*"
Rest well…

Prologue

Humpty stood out like a stripper at bible study on the corner of Seventh and F Streets in Chinatown, under the flashing red and white lights of the Verizon Center. His attire of a black Carhartt hoodie, black denim jeans, black Timberland boots and a black leather jacket screamed he was from New York City. Even though he had lived in Washington, DC for nearly a decade, his walk, talk, and hustle mentality was shaped by his place of origin.

He was getting more anxious with each passing second. He found himself pacing, or more like waddling, back and forth. Humpty wasn't just overweight; he was shaped like a giant egg.

When he was a kid, every time the "Humpty Dumpty" nursery rhyme was sang, all the other children would make fun of him. Over time, he realized it was futile to fight every child who called him Humpty Dumpty and embraced it.

Humpty was surrounded by thousands of Washington Capitals fans, all of whom rushed out of the Verizon Center, elated that their team just won the NHL Stanley Cup.

There stood Humpty. Surrounded mostly by white, overjoyed hockey fans, doing their best impersonation of the Red Sea on ecstasy. Red jerseys, red jackets, and red t-shirts. All of them kissing, hugging, and happy.

He looked at his phone. It was nearly 9:00 p.m. Almost thirty minutes past the designated meeting time. Humpty chewed on his bottom lip, a nervous tick of his.

* * *

Mixed in the crowd, Malak patiently watched Humpty's every move. He was extremely tall but knew how to act so people didn't notice him, and he blended in today by wearing a jersey.

"Aye yo! Call me back man," Humpty said into his phone, just loud enough to be heard on the other end. Capitals fans bustled passed him. He was a huge pinball within the crowd. "I know I shouldn't be doing this shit alone, but they was talkin' fifty thousand for this kind of info. Fam, I had to do it."

He paused to look up and down Seventh Street and the adjacent F Street.

"Look, this dude ain't show yet. Just in case there are any surprises, I took all the usual precautions. At least I think I did. The video is running now. I got it set up to record for a full hour after the drop time and then automatically shoot the digital file to the email. If this dude tries anything funny, I got him."

Malak smiled at how events were unfolding. Humpty thought he had protected himself from foul play. When in truth, he was bait.

Malak had watched Humpty as he scanned the crowded corner before stashing a small digital recording device in the potted bushes directly across the street from the drop spot. In fact, Malak now sat on the bench right next to it.

He watched Humpty pace back and forth, navigating his way through the crowd that erupted out of the Verizon Center. He watched Humpty bob his head and assumed he was listening to music. He didn't move when 8:30 p.m. came and went. He sat and he watched.

Once thirty minutes had passed, he looked in the direction of the recording device, back at Humpty, and thought to himself, *It's show time.* He grabbed the navy blue Jansen backpack nestled next to him and headed over.

By the time he crossed the street, Humpty was sticking his iPhone back into his pocket. Malak approached Humpty and asked, "Do you have the time?"

Humpty didn't bother to look up. He rolled his eyes and replied without making eye contact. "Nah homie." Humpty turned away from him, already moving on.

Malak didn't budge. "But I just saw you put your phone in your pocket." He grabbed the backpack from around his shoulder, held it directly in front of Humpty and repeated, "are you sure you don't…" He swung the bag like a pendulum, "have the time?"

Humpty gave an intense side glance at Malak and frowned. "What is this? And who the hell are you?" He took a couple of steps forward. It was clear the stranger's six foot, four-inch frame didn't intimidate Humpty.

Malak stepped in closer to whisper, "I'm a man holding a backpack containing ten stacks of fifty dollar bills. One hundred bills in each stack. That's fifty thousand dollars, exactly what you asked for."

Humpty gave Malak a perplexed look, and Malak could see the wheels turning in Humpty's head. Malak didn't fit the description of the person Humpty was waiting on, in any way. He was nowhere near short and squat. He towered over Humpty. He wore a Washington Capitals jersey, and was even built like he could have played for the team. He had the height and looked to be every bit of two hundred and thirty pounds. His face was spot-on too, all the way down to the scraggly hair and crooked nose.

Humpty started biting his bottom lip as sweat broke out on his forehead.

"I know you were expecting someone else. He couldn't make the meeting. Instead of rescheduling, my boss figured you wanted your money and he certainly wants what you have. You do have it, right?"

"Umm. Yeah I do! But this ain't how I do business. This ain't how I get down."

"So you don't want the money then? My boss will be very dissatisfied if this deal isn't done," Malak responded in a disappointed tone.

"Nah, that's not what I'm saying." Humpty said, "I just like to know what's going on. To protect myself man."

"Ah, yes. Protection. We all need that."

And it happened in a flash. Humpty hadn't asked to see the money. Malak hadn't asked to see the flash drive. And why would he? He'd been watching Humpty long enough to know that it was hidden in his right boot, near the ankle.

Reaching in the bag, Malak yanked out a machete. He dropped the bag while driving the blade lightning-quick into Humpty's stomach. Humpty burped a scream as blood erupted. With the surrounding noise, no one immediately reacted. They didn't notice right away that they were in the middle of a murder. Some were rushing off to the bar for an after-game drink. The most tired of the crowd were rolling toward the stairs and escalators to make the next train home. While others were stuffed onto a sidewalk about to burst at its seam, simply enjoying the victory of the night. All present, to a certain extent, but preoccupied.

And *slice.* That was all it took. Humpty's insides slopped out of his belly. That finally caught peoples' attention. He fell back against the wall behind him and slid to the ground.

Malak knew he had to move quickly. Still holding the bag, he bent over Humpty and went straight for his prize—the flash drive in his right boot. He straightened and walked around the corner to make his way back across the street, heading south on Seventh Street. Before placing the bloodied machete back in the bag, Malak dumped the money in the intersection as he crossed.

Pandemonium. As Humpty sat dying against a wall, a crowd of Washington Capitals fans scrounged around for fifty-dollar bills flying throughout the street. Traffic stopped. People fought over money. Humpty sat there dying. And Malak walked away in a game jersey. Lost in the crowd.

Chapter 1

"And where the hell do you think you're going?"

Who knew this question would reshape the nature of our relationship? The question, itself, was born out of fear. I certainly had no idea that its answer would change my life.

I sat on a pink bench as cold as the mint chocolate chip ice cream I scooped into my mouth. Coco sat directly across from me with her little sister Latonya next to her.

We were enjoying after-bowling treats of Baskin-Robbins ice cream, and between the three of us, we were eating all thirty-one flavors. Since the bill was on me, it was like they were an ice cream eating tag-team, intent on breaking my pockets. Served me right for talking smack about beating Coco at the lanes. Better yet, that's what I got for betting Coco that I would win. Loser buys the ice cream for everyone.

The problem was that Coco never mentioned she was a nationally ranked bowler while away at college. *Childhood friends shouldn't hide important things from each other*, I thought to myself, after losing horribly. But a deal was a deal and I had to pay up.

"You see your mom yet?" Coco asked.

"Not since her birthday," I said, hoping the discussion would end there.

"Jeez! That was two months ago."

"She'll be ok," I said. I shifted in my seat and purposely avoided eye contact, hoping she'd take the hint.

She didn't. "You can't blame her, you know. It's not her fault," Coco said as she began rummaging through the handbag sitting on her lap. "Hey, call my phone. I can't find it anywhere."

"Wish I could help. Phone is at the crib. Damn thing won't hold a charge. It's been plugged up for nearly a year," I said, welcoming the change of topic.

Before I could blink, Latonya whipped out her brand new iPhone 6. "You can use mine," she said, sliding her phone along the table to Coco.

"Thank you, baby," Coco said. I never understood kids with these expensive cell phones. Ten years old, with a cell phone fancier than mine. Coco dialed her number and a synthetic chime rang from the bottom of her bag.

Even while sitting, anyone could see that Coco had a body other women would kill for and men would manipulate to possess. She could have been a model if she wanted. But not those stick-figure women that floated down the catwalks of Milan. I'm talking the XXL, Maxim, and FHM type of model. The ones with beauty, body, and in Coco's case, a basket full of brains. She was probably the smartest person I knew.

Her soft brown skin was blemish free. Coco was a name made perfect for her. Not a nickname either. Her mother named her Coco after taking one look at her perfectly colored complexion straight out of the womb.

No one made a sound. It could have been the ice cream high we were experiencing. I just watched her in silence and enjoyed my emerald-green treat. At least, as much as I could before the madness started.

Suddenly a loud crash of glass could be heard coming from the front of the store. Coco and I stretched our necks in that direction to see what the commotion was about. I stared in disbelief.

Goddamnit! That fool is holding a gun!

Two gunmen stood at the front of the shop, imposing their will. The glass display of new ice cream flavors was shattered in an attempt to startle the lone worker at the cash register. We were in the middle of an old-fashion stickup.

They didn't see us yet. We were at the end of a long display counter, three stations over in the final booth. The moment Coco and I figured out the deal, we all ducked down in the booth to the point where our bodies were nearly under the table.

The robber who stood at the door seemed to be the strong but silent type. I watched him twist the door handle to make sure it was locked, before resuming his guard duties.

"I don't want to hurt you," the other man said, pointing his gun at the cashier. "But I will, you understand?"

For effect, Mr. Strong and Quiet pulled a gun out of his pocket and held it down the side of his body.

Before he was even asked, the worker opened the cash register and stepped to his right. Mr. Strong and Quiet didn't seem comfortable with that particular move and extended his gun toward the cashier. "Put your hands up and step away from the counter. Let's play it safe," he said.

My main concern was keeping us out of their line of-sight. Coco and I crouched low enough to keep hidden even though I had an angle where I could periodically peek out without getting caught. And then I remembered something. I wasn't psychic, but I knew exactly what was about to happen next.

The man who scooped the ice cream had retreated to an office or room behind the cashier at the register. It only made sense to me that he was completely oblivious to the robbery that was taking place.

"Coco," I whispered. She didn't respond, wiping ice cream from the mouth of the little girl. I lightly tapped the table and whispered to her again. "Coco!"

She looked up at me. I had never seen that type of fear in her eyes. She had a hand on Latonya's head to reassure her.

"Listen," I lipped, trying to be as quiet as possible. "One man scooped our ice cream. But I paid someone else." I reached across the table and grabbed her hand in an effort to console and coach her at the same time. "Whatever happens, I need you to stay calm."

A door swung open. "Hey Johnny! Did you—" Two shots rang out from Mr. Strong and Quiet's gun. From my hidden space, I was able to see the force of the shots lift him off his feet. He flew backwards into the office.

The sound of the gunfire was too much for Coco to handle. A yelp of, "Oh my God!" slipped out as she pulled Latonya closer. The sound of the gun frightened the little girl as well. I couldn't tell if Coco grabbed her to protect her or because she felt like she needed protection herself.

Her reaction certainly alerted the robbers to our presence.

"Go check it out," Mr. Strong and Quiet barked to the other. As it turned out, he seemed not to be so quiet after all. I could hear the other gunman walking closer, so I made up my mind to do the only thing I thought might save our lives. Either that or prolong the inevitable.

"Stay here," I said to Coco.

"Stay here?" she asked. She reached out and grabbed my arm. "And where the hell do you think you're going?"

Chapter 2

"Don't shoot!"

It was all I could think to yell. I emerged from my hidden alcove, shaking off Coco's gasp. Hands raised way above my head. If I could convince the gunman we weren't a threat and would keep our mouths shut, maybe he'd let us leave.

As I stood up, I spied an emergency exit behind our booth. If I had noticed it earlier, I would have just grabbed everybody and made a run for it.

This was my first good look at the man. From a distance, I underestimated his muscular girth. His arms, chest, and legs bulged to the point where his clothes stretched beyond their regular form.

"Look man. We're not going to be any trouble. I have a woman and a kid. We can slide right out that door and forget all about tonight," I said.

"What the fuck you mean 'forget about tonight'?" he asked. "I'm supposed to just let you walk the fuck out of here?"

I understood his apprehension to my proposition. Here he was committing armed robbery and his accomplice kills a man in the process. Would I let us go? That question lingered in my mind. But if I didn't try something we were certainly next to die.

"What the hell's going on back there?" Mr. Strong and Quiet yelled from the front. I heard him emptying the cash register. "Cap them mutherfuckas. We've gotta go!"

Witnesses. That's what we were. And as the old saying goes, "Dead men tell no tales."

"Look, just let us go. We won't say a word. Promise," Coco yelled from beneath the table.

With his gun trained on me, he eyed Coco. It felt like forever. If he turned his barrel toward her, I readied myself to leap between them if bullets began to fly. My heartbeat quickened. It pumped as fast as the flutter of hummingbird wings. I wasn't going to let him kill any of us without a fight.

When he finally turned his attention back to me, there was a different look in his eyes. He squinted out of one eye and cocked his head to the side.

"Anthony Ribisi?" he asked in an investigative manner. I didn't say anything in return, so he leaned in to take a closer look. "Yeah. It's you alright," he continued in a matter-of-fact-tone.

In that moment, another loud *POP* came from the front of the store, followed by the distinct sound of a body falling to the floor. The house cleaning part of the robbery. Why leave witnesses to a robbery and murder, right? Only another minute before bullets made their way toward the three of us. It was now, do or die. Time to change his mind, or else.

"I've got money. A lot of it." We focused on each other. I left no quiver in my voice. "Let the girl and kid go, and I'll take you and your man to it right now."

I could see his mind weighing the options. But a flash of light in my direction stopped everything. Blood splattered everywhere. Warmth soaked my shirt. I looked down to see crimson.

I looked back up at the gunman, confused, and watched as his body hit the floor.

Chapter 3

Officers and homicide detectives were crawling throughout the scene of the crime. Taking pictures. Interviewing potential witnesses. But it was useless. In my opinion, there wasn't a need to interview witnesses when the assailants were dead. The both of them.

During the frantic activity of the investigation, I overheard the responding officer describe what happened to one of the detectives. While Mr. Strong and Quiet focused on cleaning out the cash register, he didn't notice the cashier reach into a hidden wall compartment and retrieve the store's Smith and Wesson revolver. It was kept there specifically for robbery attempts.

The first sound of a body dropping was Mr. Strong and Quiet after getting popped at close range. The cashier crept close enough to then shoot the guy pointing his gun at me. That's what happened. He was the hero of the night.

It'd been a long day, and it wasn't anywhere close to being over. I had a terrified friend and a child to calm down. The thought dawned on me that Latonya's mother hadn't bothered to check in with us, at the very least to see why her daughter hadn't returned home. And it was approaching midnight.

I wasn't really surprised. It reminded me of my own childhood experience. My mother worked three jobs; a fulltime day job, part-time night job, and an on-call weekend position. It kept her preoccupied and out of the home. You do what you must when the bills need to be paid.

I figured Latonya dealt with something similar or maybe even worse.

We were done with the cops and I had everyone loaded into the car, I sat on the hood, finishing my cigarette. It didn't seem like anyone had anything else to ask us. I took one last pull off the Newport and walked around to the driver side door.

Through the activity of the night, I heard a familiar voice.

"Well I'll be damned! If it ain't Anthony Ribisi, live and in the flesh? Who would've guessed you'd be anywhere near this mess?"

I heard nothing but condescension, but turned to engage him anyway. He was of average height. No, maybe below average. His smart mouth contradicted his unassuming and modest stature.

"I'm sorry?" I said as he walked closer to car.

"Anthony, right? You must not remember me." He extended his hand and even though I didn't want to, I shook it. "Detective Che Aguilar. We met about five years ago when I was working the Organize Crime Unit."

"Is that so?" But I remembered him. I remembered that I didn't like him.

"I'm homicide now and since this is a homicide, I had to be here to do my detective thing."

"Well. Do you need anything from me? Detective," I added. I'm not sure if I could've rolled my eyes any harder.

"I don't right now. But let's chat in the morning. I bet you know where the station is, right? Let's say nine o'clock."

"Sounds good. I need to get them home," I said as I climbed into the car.

"Okay. That's cool man, no problem. I need to run downtown anyway." Aguilar leaned into the open window. "I've gotta see what's up with this fat boy that was carved up. Cut the fucker's guts right on outta him."

Detective Aguilar only then noticed Latonya sleeping in the back. "Oh Jeez. My bad man, I hope she didn't hear me. Well, go handle your biz Anthony. I'll see you tomorrow."

The detective stepped away from the vehicle, allowing me to roll up the window, hit the gas, and pull off. Between the girl being fast asleep and Coco still in shock, the car was filled with complete silence.

We got about a half a mile down the road before Coco turned to me. "Anthony?" she asked. "Why was everyone calling you Anthony tonight?"

I didn't bother to look in her direction, but she didn't need any acknowledgement from me in order to continue.

"Jelani! Do you wanna tell me who the hell Anthony Ribisi is and why everyone thinks you're him?"

I just drove. She waited nearly a minute for a response.

"Jelani!"

All I could do was stare ahead at the road and give her a simple three-word answer.

"No. I don't."

Chapter 4

After taking Latonya home, Coco and I rolled to a stop in front of my apartment, where her car sat. There was a definite contrast between the 1998 Chevy Malibu I drove and Coco's 2012 Mercedes-Benz C250 Coupe. Since college she had done pretty well for herself.

Although not a complete rust bucket, my car wasn't the freshest thing on the road. But in my opinion, the rust on the fenders gave it character. The dents on the hood meant she had been battled tested, and the scratches and scrapes along her body were merely scars, the result of being wounded in war.

My car felt like a perfect representation of me. The only difference was that I knew how to keep my rust, dents, and scars covered, hidden from sight and protected from those who I didn't trust. Which included most people.

I got out and walked around to Coco's door to let her out. Something I learned from Marco. "Never let a woman open a door, pick up a dropped item, or light a cigarette in your presence," he always said. "Little actions go a long way. If you do this, women will feel respected. They'll see you as a man willing to protect them."

I listen to Marco when he tells me something. Man, was he right. Aside from feeling respected and protected, it was a sure-fire way to get their bra unhooked. I followed his advice with every woman around me. And I tried to be consistent too: fat, skinny, pretty, or ugly. It didn't matter to me. If Marco said do it, it was done. But was it wrong that every once and awhile I used this golden nugget of knowledge for the dark side? I didn't think so.

I walked Coco to her car door in silence, both of us exhausted. After kissing her on the cheek and opening her car door, I waited for her to hop in.

"Wait a minute!" Coco gave me an incredulous look and broke the silence. "So we're really not going to talk?"

"It's been a long day. Aren't you tired?"

"I am, Jelani. But it's not just that. I am tired. God, I'm exhausted!" Her volume went up with every word. "But I'm also curious and I'm angry and I'm terrified!" I closed the car door as it became apparent that she wasn't getting in the vehicle any time soon.

"And then I look at you," she continued. "Nothing. You're your usual 'cool as a popsicle' self. And to my recollection, we almost died tonight! You almost died! But there's nothing coming from you. Nothing!"

I took a step away from Coco. I didn't know why. Maybe I hoped it would diffuse the situation and calm her down. But Coco saw right through my evasive move and didn't fall for it. She moved in to ensure that we were looking into each other's eyes and cupped my face between her warm, soft hands so I couldn't avoid eye contact.

"Jelani, I know you've been hurt and that your life has been rough, but you can't do this. You can't bury things. You've got to learn to express yourself."

"Who says I need expressing? I'm not a client and this ain't one of your therapy sessions. Why don't you get in your car, go home, and get some rest. We can—"

"Talk about this tomorrow," Coco said. "That's the problem. There's never a tomorrow. We've been friends since twelve years old and every time we start talking about anything remotely emotional, you want to talk about it tomorrow. Well, I'm still waiting for tomorrow. And damnit, tonight you almost..." It seemed as if Coco couldn't finish.

"I'm good," I said. "You don't have to worry about me." I pulled her in and held her.

"No. You're not good. And I do worry." There was silence for a few moments. *This was it*, I thought to myself. Time to get her in the car and on the road.

But Coco pushed away from me, ready to go in for round two. There was a fire lit in her eyes.

"And at least two different times someone called you a name that I've *never* heard. You didn't flinch or budge. You never corrected anyone, either. So I'm thinking that other name is one you're used to being called. You know what that tells me? You have a-whole-nother life that I know nothing about. And we've known each other since twelve years old!" She made her point with three firm jabs into my chest. "So don't tell me you're good, Jelani. Or is it Anthony?"

"Are you done?" I asked.

"No," She paused. "Yes. Maybe. I was scared that I was going to lose you. And tonight helped me realize how much I don't want that to happen."

She walked back into my embrace. It was something about the way we stood there and held each other. Like the calm after a turbulent storm. She held me tighter than she had in the past. More intense.

I didn't want to argue with her. Every word out of her mouth was true. I'd locked people out. Pushed people away. Had yet to have a happy and fulfilling relationship. And Coco had a ringside seat to the prizefight of my life. Like she said, "since twelve years old."

Even worse, there were things about me that were foreign to her. Yes, we were friends for almost our whole lives, but nevertheless, I would never be able to share with her all the things I'd done. Or the things I'm still capable of doing.

"Well, it's clear you're not trying to get in this car and go anywhere. Do you want to come up?" I asked.

"Wait a minute. I get a little saucy and now you're trying to take advantage of me?"

"No hun. I'm just trying to give you options."

Coco leaned back within my hug and cracked a huge smile, her first since the madness of the night. And it was beautiful. "You behave yourself there. Men have to earn this. I'm a good girl."

"What a shame," I said. As soon as the words left my mouth, Coco leaned in and kissed me. Her lips were softer than her hands. I loosened my grip in order to hold her more gently. I've wanted this women my entire adult life, and here we were, finally locked in a lover's embrace, sharing a passionate kiss.

I've opened all of her doors. She's dropped books, keys, hats, and gloves, never having to bend or stoop to pick anything up. Not once. I'd used Marco's advice to manipulate many women into liking me, but not Coco. It didn't hit me until we kissed: Coco required something more. She needed a gun thrust in my face to awaken our slumbered attraction. Who knew that a near death experience was more effective than chivalry?

I couldn't wait to tell Marco.

* * *

From the inside of his car, he was close enough to see them, but not enough to hear their conversation. He watched Anthony and the unidentified woman walk to her car. He took pictures while they argued, hugged, kissed. The two of them walked arm-in-arm up the front stairs to Anthony's apartment building.

He took caution to remain inconspicuous. Neither Anthony nor his female friend seemed to notice him watching them through his telephoto lens—and why would they? He was good at what he did. As the duo walked into the building, he placed his camera down and surveyed the neighborhood. No witnesses. He grabbed the handgun sitting in the passenger seat and reached for his door handle, but the three buzzes from his phone stopped him.

He picked up the phone and said, "Yeah. I'm going in."

He listened for a moment or two as the person on the other end spoke. "Are you sure? I can go in and get him now, chick or no chick."

The man lit a cigarette and continued to listen to the marching orders.

"Whatever you say. It's your show," he said and hung up.

And with that, he started his car, pulled out of his parking space, and headed down the street. He stopped in front of Anthony's building long enough to take in the surroundings and pulled off.

Chapter 5

Who is Anthony Ribisi? The question of the night. I leaned against the archway of the kitchen and watched Coco help herself to the last bottle of Corona Light I had in the fridge.

"Do you mind?" she asked, out of obligation, though it didn't matter because she had already grabbed the bottle and was removing the cap as she closed the door.

"Not at all." The only reason I kept Corona Light was for her and she knew it. I, personally, couldn't stand the beer. She brushed past me and I watched her make her way to the sofa, kicking off her shoes in the process. This was a normal routine.

The sofa was her territory. Romance between us was non-existent. We had been friends for so long. I wondered that since we just stretched the limits of our relationship, maybe this was the night she would graduate from sleeping on the sofa to sleeping in the bed. With me.

In truth, I knew better. So long as there were unanswered identity questions, it wouldn't happen. Anthony Ribisi was a mystery to her and for the first time I thought about sharing what I really did for the Ribisi family. But how could I without scaring the hell out of her or pushing her away?

Coco reached over for the remote. "Do you still have *Coming to America* on DVR for me? I need something to take my mind off of tonight."

She knew I did. Like the beer, I only keep it for her. She found the movie, hit the play button, and curled her body into the corner of the sofa.

Coco watched the movie, but was distracted.

At this point, the risk wasn't about losing the opportunity to sleep with someone I'd wanted to have since forever. Losing a cherished friend was the real risk. There was no way she'd understand.

Or then again, maybe she would. Being a therapist, I was certain she was trained in dealing with multiple personalities. While this wasn't the same thing, I felt like Jelani and Anthony were two distinct personalities. They were opposite sides of the same cruddy coin.

Tonight, I was Jelani Jones. Enjoying a night of fun and bowling with a dear friend and a child, eating dessert at an ice cream shop as if I was a normal human being.

While six months ago, I was Anthony Ribisi. Sitting in a dark corner of a private room at The Macombo Lounge, a strip club on Georgia Avenue. It was the last time I had done any work on behalf of the family.

* * *

The main room of the matchbox-sized strip club was busting at the seams, as always. But the private room had a lot more space, and far fewer people. A blonde Latina named Spanish Fly walked by and offered me a lap dance. Her over-sized hips and large backside made up for her lack of breasts. Usually I didn't get lap dances, but this night was different.

I didn't want to look out of place, so I sipped a drink and accepted. I'd be lying if I said I didn't enjoy the dance, but that wasn't my purpose.

The only other patron in the private room had finished his dance and exited through a curtain of purple beads that hung in the double doorway separating the private and main rooms. As he walked out, Tommy Styles stumbled in.

"China! Get your ass back here," he yelled.

A light-skinned stripper trailed in seconds after. No taller than five feet, she was all ass and titties. Her slanted dark eyes betrayed her black and Asian heritage. Blasian is what they just started calling this specific ethnic mix.

China pushed Tommy back onto the couch across the room from me and straddled him. Grinding up and down to the music. Tommy showered China with twenty-dollar bills. Twenty-dollar bills that I believed he took from the bank at one of Marco's gambling houses.

Tommy was hired to run cash between the bank and the tables. And when money started to come up short, a closer eye was placed on him to ensure he wasn't slipping some into his pocket during the transport. After a month of observation, I spied Tommy stealing the money. It started with a twenty-dollar bill here and there. Then it became stacks of twenty-dollar bills periodically throughout a night.

Once I brought this to Marco's attention, he told me to do what I thought would be best in order to rectify the situation. I felt a meeting was in order.

It was no secret that Tommy enjoyed strip clubs in general and The Macombo Lounge in particular. So with his newfound fortune, I knew he'd be there.

I paid Spanish Fly for her service along with a hefty tip and made my way over to Tommy. While he was preoccupied with China, I sat on the edge of the couch they were on.

Tommy was leaned back with China pressed against him, her massive boobs in his face. Tommy was in heaven, but he had enough presence of mind to notice he had company.

"Hey, beat it buddy. This ain't a peep show," Tommy said.

I didn't respond.

"I said scram," he yelled, finally looking at me.

Once he recognized me, his tone did a complete turnaround.

"Oh geez! I didn't know that was you, Anthony. I'm sorry, man. What are you doing here? You seem like the type that would be at one of those fancy places like Stadium," he joked.

I still didn't say a word. I looked at China and nodded my head toward the door. She seemed to know it was time for her to leave. As she walked away, Tommy looked at me, then back at her.

"Hey, babe. Where you going?" He forced a laugh along with his false light tone.

Once she was clear of the room, I leaned over and picked up one of the dropped bills from the floor.

"You've been spending an awful lot of money here, Tommy. I'm going to ask you a question and I'm only going to ask you once. If you're honest, I might be able to help you out. If you're not..."

Tommy looked at the money I had in my hand as beads of sweat formed on his brow. He swallowed hard enough that it could be heard over the dampened music coming through from the club.

"Where'd you get this money?"

"I...I... Why are you asking? I work for Marco. You know that, man. All the money I spend here is what I'm paid."

What Tommy didn't know was that I stamped all of the money he transported with fluorescent ink that could only be seen under a blacklight: a large *X* over Andrew Jackson's face.

I held up the bill that was already in my hand and pulled a blacklight pen from my pocket. I waved the pen over the bill and watched as the *X* illuminated from the bill. I folded and placed it in my pocket, along with the pen.

Fear spread across Tommy's face. He was caught and he knew it. I got up from the sofa and walked to the beaded curtain separating the rooms.

"Come on. It's time to go."

Tommy knew what that meant. The moment he walked out of that club, he would never see it again. He would never see his friends again. His family would mourn his disappearance.

"No," Tommy said. He looked around the room, possibly for another way out. An emergency exit maybe. "I'm not going anywhere! What are you gonna do? Kill me in a club full of witnesses?"

"No. I'm not."

I ripped the purple beads all the way back. Tommy's eyes widened in disbelief. The other room was as empty as ours. The music was still playing, but the DJ was gone.

The bartenders were gone. The other club goers had vanished. China, Spanish Fly, and every other dancer were also gone. We were the only ones left in The Macombo Lounge.

"Let's go, Tommy. I don't wanna have to carry the dead weight."

***

It was two weeks before anyone saw Tommy again. His lifeless body was found in a green waste management dumpster off of Route One in Laurel, Maryland. The leather strap used to suffocate and snap his neck was still wrapped around his throat.

Who is Anthony Ribisi? A garbage man, if you will. Or better yet, a mediator. He is someone who intervenes between conflicting parties to promote the resolution of a grievance.

I watched Coco. And she watched the Prince of Zamunda. She didn't have a smile on her face. She was nowhere near laughing.

It was clear to me…Coco would never understand.

Chapter 6

It was nine thirty the next morning when I walked into Marco's Italian Restaurant on the historic U Street corridor of Washington, DC. This area had become prime location over the years. Once a dilapidated and burned down artery, U Street had gone through the gentrification that had become prevalent in urban areas from city to city.

U Street was all but completely destroyed when the riots took hold of the city. After Martin Luther King, Jr. was assassinated, all hell broke loose. But what a lot of present day, new era Washingtonians didn't know was that U Street thrived before the riots. All they knew were the crack houses and prostitutes because it was the only thing they saw when they moved to town. But before that, U Street was called the Black Broadway. That's a part of what made it historic.

From the Howard Theatre on one end to the Lincoln Theatre at the other, a Who's Who of Jazz and Rhythm & Blues artists entertained the crowds for decades. The actress and singer Pearl Bailey coined the phrase Black Broadway. The great Duke Ellington even grew up in the shadows of the U Street Corridor on Thirteenth Street, only a block away. And it was the largest black community in the country, until the Harlem explosion in the 1920's. So U Street was special. And Marco Ribisi knew it.

Marco also made sure that we all knew it as well. His children and his staff, who were one and the same at times, as well as anyone who had an affiliation with Marco's Restaurant.

Upon walking in, you would find pictures of the Rat Pack next to pictures of the Temptations. A portrait of James Brown hung aside a portrait of Frank Sinatra. On any given occasion Liza Minelli or Etta James could be heard pouring out of the house speakers.

This was what Marco wanted. A respectful and complimentary blend between his Italian American culture and history, and that of the community he did business with. Of all the music and art that adorned the walls, his favorite was a mural that stretched the length of the eatery. It depicted the scene of the famous I Have A Dream speech given by Martin Luther King, Jr. But instead of the historical backdrop of the Lincoln Memorial, Marco had the artist place the good doctor and his throngs of listeners in front of the Valle d'Aosta. It was one of the most well known mountainous valleys in all of Italy.

When I walked in, the first person I saw was Jena Ribisi standing behind the bar, counting bottles of bourdon. She was dressed in all black, which was standard bartender attire. Her clothes showed off a ballerina body. And even though she was fully covered, her neckline, hands and face glowed from a natural, year round, and olive colored tan.

"Think I could get a..."

"Maker's Mark on the rocks." She turned around with a note pad and ink pen in her hand. "Don't you think it's too early for that?" She chided.

"You might as well give it to him, sis." A voice came from behind me. I turned my head to see Jena's twin brother Johnnie standing at the door, which led to his father's office.

He was the spitting image of Jena, except he had a stocky frame. It was the result of playing football from the youth leagues, all the way through high school. "You didn't think we'd miss you for six months. The old man is gonna be pissed. What've you been doing? Playing in those dirty alleyways?"

Turning my attention back to Jena. "Ooh! I'm in trouble. You heard the man." I slapped my hand down on the bar top. "Wet me up, my good lady!"

"And for the record," I said to Johnnie, "The old man has taught me well. Some of my best work is done in those dirty alleyways."

Jena grabbed the bottle of alcohol and poured a little out. "I'll give you a shot, for now."

"Your brother says I was missed. Ti sono mancato?" *Did you miss me?* I asked.

Jena and I loved each other like brother and sister, but every once in awhile, there was some harmless flirting.

She rolled her eyes and replied. "Il tuo accento ha bisogno di aiuto." *Your accent needs help.*

"Don't blame me. You've had a lifetime to teach me right!" I yelled as I dashed away. I was her personal language arts project for more than a decade. Jena loved her family's native tongue and felt that since I was a part of the family, it would be good for me to speak it too.

Johnnie was still holding the door. He and I weren't as close as I was with Jena, but I saw him as my brother nevertheless.

"What are you gonna tell the old man? And we heard you knocked off a couple of robbers last night."

I laughed and patted him on the back. "You've got me confused with an ice cream clerk. And stay out of my business?" I joked.

We both entered Marcos' office to find Marco seated at his desk, with Dominic Nicholas, "Nick Nick" seated on the other side of his desk in one of the two empty chairs.

The two men had styles that were in contrast. Marco was blue collar. Scruffy and worn. His chin was full of stubble. But Nick Nick was corporate and clean cut. His sharpness was underscored by his perfectly placed hair and manicured nails.

Nick Nick was Marco's right-hand man. His consigliore, if you will. But in the case of the Ribisi organization, there was no Underboss to complete a three-person administration. Marco and Nick Nick conspired to make a majority, if not all of the decisions. Marco was in charge and there was no doubt who was in charge in his absence.

Nick Nick was smart as a whip, as cold as ice, and as viscous as a bull. He was refined but brutal. But he was also getting old.

Maybe that's why Marco had him train me. I had been by his side, watching and learning since finishing high school. It was apparent to Marco that Nick Nick and I had a gift for the same kind of work. And he was the best teacher that I could have had.

In fact, it was Nick Nick's idea to use my middle name with the family and when conducting business. It kept people off guard when anticipating a meet up with "Anthony," from the Ribisi family, as opposed to a brother named Jelani Jones. It made it easier for us to exercise a level or discretion and to take advantage of situations, when needed.

"Sit down." Marco commanded, so I did. "How'd you enjoy your vacation?"

"Ah." I shrugged. "I didn't know what to do with myself."

"Six months is a long time to be bored," Marco said.

"It certainly is, Pop!" Johnnie yelled from a chair, behind me, near the door.

"Thanks son. I got this!" He shouted back while holding up his hand.

Johnnie still didn't know what was going on. He didn't know that my leave of absence wasn't unexplained or unexpected. Marco was a strategist. He was a planner. And the past six months was a part of a bigger plan. We could never fully understand the method behind Marco's thinking. Nobody really could. At least, not until the entire plan was unveiled. So it was no surprise that what he said next blindsided the hell out of us.

Chapter 7

Detective Aguilar sat at his desk reading through the police report from Humpty's murder. Crime scene and autopsy photos were spread out over his desk.

"Can someone grab me that printout from the phone company?" He seemed to yell through the department, but not to anyone specifically.

"You're welcome," his partner, Sam Daniels said, slapping the fax from the cell phone company down on the desk. The pressure from his massive hand almost split the desk in two. "Oh, wait a minute. You never thanked me."

Sam Daniels had been Aguilar's partner for the last two years. This odd couple had known each other nearly their whole lives but each entered the police force and became detectives at different times. Daniels was nearly twice the size of Aguilar.

They were local boys. Growing up in the same Trinidad neighborhood in the Northeast section of Washington, DC, and attending high school together fostered a natural bond between the two. They were more than partners, they were like brothers.

"Stop being a creampuff." Aguilar was short in his tone.

"Whaddya got there?" Daniels asked, fingering through the photos on the desk.

"I'm just making sure I'm not missing anything." Aguilar handed Daniels the photographs.

"Ok? What am I looking at?" Daniels sighed.

"Figures." Aguilar said. "I thought I was working with a real cop."

"Whatever. Why don't you follow up on some real leads?"

"On some real leads?" Aguilar chuckled to himself.

"Did you even look at the phone company printout? My God! Do I have to do everything?"

Aguilar looked down at the sheet, still lying on his desk. He reached for it, but by that time Daniels snatched it up.

"You see this phone number with the Maryland area code? Look at the amount of times Humpty called it in the three days leading up to his untimely demise. You'd think the number belonged to a close friend or family member, right? But that number can't be traced to a person. It's a disposable. A burner."

"Ok. Dead end."

"Maybe." Daniels said. "Maybe not. But if you look at the phone number at the bottom of the page, it's the one with the Washington, DC area code. That's the very last number our boy called, before getting ya know, disemboweled."

Daniels waited a moment for Aguilar to catch up to him.

"Well that number, my good man, can be linked to someone. And do you see who?"

Aguilar's eyes widen with excitement.

It was a lead.

"You've gotta be fucking kidding me." Aguilar muttered.

Daniels felt pretty good about himself. "So. You wanna thank me now?"

Chapter 8

"As everyone knows, Anthony's been gone for the last six months." Marco said. "But everyone doesn't know why."

Of course, that statement wasn't completely true. Nick Nick knew everything. He and Marco didn't keep secrets from each other. It was my guess he said that so his son wouldn't feel too out of the loop. In actuality, he was the only one who thought my disappearance was a result of nonfeasance.

Marco continued. "I asked Anthony to take a little hiatus. I wanted to assess how much of his services we could ultimately do without. Johnnie, you've done a fine job filling in when needed, and I thank you for that, son. But if you noticed, we've had fewer and fewer runs to the gambling houses. Most recently, we haven't made a run to the houses at all. This has meant less money from those sources and not as much need for the usual security presence.

"I've spent the last year thinking about whether this family could survive if we eliminated all streams of illegitimate income. And to be honest, we've done quite well. With that being said, I am permanently shutting down the gambling houses. It's over. Pardon the expression, but we're cashing in our chips."

Marco stopped to let the weight of his words hit Johnnie and me. Johnnie was sitting straight up in his chair. There was a look of shock that washed over his face, as it did mine. The only person who didn't look shocked by this announcement was Nick Nick.

I was in disbelief for one reason alone. It was my understanding that Marco pulled me from active duty because he was giving his son an opportunity to step in and learn the ropes of the business more intimately. But clearly that wasn't the case.

Over the past six months, Marco had been closing gambling house after gambling house in an effort to legitimize the Ribisi family. I couldn't help but wonder if we were getting the whole story. And if not, I couldn't help but wonder what the whole story was.

Just then, Johnnie shot up and walked closer to his fathers' desk. He was visibly upset with the revelation and asked exactly what I wanted to know.

"Pop. If the houses are shut down, what's the family expected to do?"

"Look around you. We have a very successful restaurant. I'm also opening a second in Georgetown and a third, next year, in downtown Silver Spring." Marco dismissively added, "We'll be fine. You and Jena will be fine."

Even though I wasn't using my mouth, nothing was wrong with my ears and my eyes. I could hear and see the subtext to Johnnie's question. He wasn't worried about what the family would do for money and how they would financially survive. Even though he didn't say it, that wasn't Johnnie's real concern.

The question Johnnie really wanted to yell was, "*What about me?!*" Johnnie had played the role of supportive son his entire life with the hopes of having the family business passed down to him one day. And now, how could that happen if the family business was no more? Johnnie didn't want to be a restaurateur; he wanted to be a crime boss.

"The other organizations and families won't let us just walk away! It doesn't happen like that!"

"Yes they will." Marco waved his hand. "They have no choice in the matter."

Johnnie looked around the room and muttered, "This is bullshit."

Marco saw value in his children's independence, so long as they weren't disrespectful. And Johnnie was walking that fine line between respect and having his teeth knocked out.

"What did you say?" Marco questioned.

Johnnie didn't say anything in return. He stood silently and stared away from his father.

"Sit down." Marco pointed to the chair. "I built this business. I decide when it's over. And gentlemen, it's a wrap!"

Marco paused to read that there was consensus on all of our faces. Everyone nodded in agreement. Even Johnnie did so begrudgingly.

"Alright. That's the bad news." Marco leaned back and folded his fingers together on the desk.

"The bad news." I chuckled, trying to lighten the air. "Well, what's the good news then?"

Nick Nick spoke for the first time. "I'm sorry, Anthony, there is no good news. There is bad news and badder news."

Even with my attempt at light humor, the room became dark and heavy. I sensed somberness. It was on everyone's face except mine. They knew something I didn't.

Nick Nick asked, "Anthony, when was the last time you talked to your good friend? Humpty."

* * *

I sat motionless for fifteen minutes and listened to Nick Nick describe the details of Humpty's murder as it was given to him. Nick Nick had a man inside the police department who periodically fed him information he thought the Ribisi family might be interested in.

It was known by a few within the department that I was affiliated with Marco, but the extent of my affiliation wasn't clear. From the outside looking in, I was the faithful employee of the restaurant, knowing the family since childhood. I was still clean-cut.

Humpty, on the other hand, had been picked up a number of times. Once for disorderly conduct, once for assault, and three times for being in possession of a leafy green substance that had an odor consistent with marijuana. Humpty was no stranger to the police. And it was also known that we were best friends. Out of courtesy, Nick Nick's connection shared everything he had about Humpty's murder, so that they could share it with me.

The thought of my brother from another mother being murdered, and in such a brutal manner, brought about a number of intense emotions. I was confused, sad, and angry. The room was spinning.

Humpty was the only person that I could trust with my inner most thoughts. And he never asked me to trust him.

Humpty was there whenever I needed him and asked nothing in return.

"I know this is a lot to process," Marco said in a low voice. "You know, we liked Humpty too. When you was on your, uh, vacation...he came in and did a little work for us. Just a little. Nothing big. He was good with us."

Even being as hurt as I was, I found it interesting that Humpty never mentioned he was doing side work with Marco. He was well aware of my connection with them. Like Marco and Nick Nick, we didn't keep secrets between us. Maybe he didn't tell me because he thought it was only temporary. Maybe he didn't want me think that he was trying to take my spot, which I would never think.

"But here's the important piece." Marco said. "We don't have the full story yet. This thing could have been a mugging gone wrong, or it could have been a hit. We don't know. So until we do, Anthony, you can't take to retaliation. You just can't."

Funny thing, I was already ten steps ahead of him. In my mind, I had already tracked down the responsible parties. I had already set their homes on fire. The echo of their funeral dirge had already rung in my ears. That's how much Humpty meant to me, and here Marco was asking, no demanding, that I sit tight.

"You know what I'm good at. You know what I do well."

"When you're thinking clear," he immediately responded. "What you do well when you are thinking clear. You cannot retaliate for two reasons."

These better be some damn good reasons.

"First off, you are angry and it's apparent. Any decision you make or action you take out of anger will not be the best course of action. You need a clear head to do what you do so well, and that you do not have."

I hated to admit it but he was absolutely right. Clearer heads always made better plans.

"And second. Let's say this is related to what we do somehow. We are about to pull out of the business, Anthony. Reacting to this will only keep the family in a way of life I'm am trying to navigate us out of. You are a part of this family. And if you happen to meet a bullet, because of some fixation on payback...well, then God help the man who pulled the trigger. Do you understand?"

I looked away and nodded my head but this time gestures weren't sufficient.

"Anthony. Tell me you understand."

It took every ounce of discipline within me to answer Marco. When it comes to Marco, I'm loyal and obedient. In all of my life, he has never steered me wrong. And at this very moment, he required that obedience once again.

"Say it!" Marco commanded.

With a tear streaming down the left side of my face, I agreed.

"I understand."

Chapter 9

How I got there, I couldn't tell you. How much time had passed since learning of my good friends' murder couldn't be determined either. But there I was, sitting on one of the benches that lined the upper quadrangle of Meridian Hill Park, which was affectionately referred to as Malcolm X Park by the residents of Chocolate City.

This is where it all started for Humpty and I. And it felt like I had been transported through time.

Looking across fields of faded grass, I could see a group of twelve and thirteen year old boys playing a game of tackle football. It felt funny looking at the twelve year old version of me. I had grown so much since then, I was unrecognizable. My arms and legs were thin and I had a pretty big head for my size.

There were five boys on my team and five on the other. I say "my" team, but in truth, Joe Mittens was the leader of the team. And no one challenged him for that distinction. He was bigger, stronger, and faster than the rest of us.

Joe called all the plays when we were in our huddle. It wasn't anything sophisticated like you'd hear in a real football huddle. No one used numbers or words like boot, gut or waggle. Joe would just say, "Run to the right and I'll throw you the ball."

It was simple and easy. But I liked playing on defense back then. It was far more fun to tackle and try to take the ball away, as opposed to running and avoiding a hit. Even as a young person, I enjoyed confrontation. I enjoyed the hitting. Maybe a little too much.

The other team had the ball and prepared to hike it. I crept up to the line of scrimmage expecting the quarterback to drop back and attempt a pass. He looked kind of slow throughout the game and had only grown more tired over time. To me, this only meant that if he dropped back for another pass, he was mine. And that's exactly what happened.

He hiked the ball and ran back about three yards. He wanted to go back even more, but I was too fast for him. Barely anyone blocked me. He couldn't find anyone open for the ball, and I threw my body and arms at him. The only problem was that Joe's cousin Frankie had the same idea.

We both reached the quarterback at the same time. I hit him high and Frankie hit him low. When we collided, the quarterback let out a scream between the two of us. But as we met at the poor boy, because of our body positions, Frankie's head collided with my knee.

When the dust had cleared, both the quarterback and Frankie were lying on the ground. The quarterback got up and shook it off, but Frankie just lied there rolling in agony. It was clear he wouldn't finish the rest of the game.

Humpty sat on the benches and watched the whole thing. He had just moved to DC from New York a few weeks earlier and always made his way to the park in an attempt to make new friends. It hadn't been working too well for him. I looked over at the lonely boy and thought this would be a good opportunity to get him into the game and maybe make some new friends.

"Time-out!" I yelled. I walked over to Joe. "Hey Joe. Looks like your cousin's done. We need another player."

"Why'd you call time-out?" Joe asked. "This ain't your team, man."

"Your cuz got the shit knocked outta him and we need a new man." By this time I waved Humpty off of the bench and he was walking closer to Joe and me. "Just calm down and let's play some ball." I handed the football to Joe and walked over to Humpty.

"Fuck you and fuck fatboy!" Joe shouted.

There was a chorus of "Oohs!" that came from the other neighborhood boys. By this time everyone had forgotten about Frankie, who was sitting up on the ground and shaking his head. The guys now gathered around Joe and I. It was like they smelled a fight in the air.

I couldn't understand why Joe was so angry. Did I disrespect his authority by calling the time-out? Or maybe he was upset because I knocked his cousin out. I couldn't place it. But that was now beside the point, no matter what his issue was, I wasn't going to let him talk to me in a reckless manner. That's how people begin to think you're weak.

If I let Joe yell and curse me out now, who's to say he wouldn't do it again? Worse yet, it would also open the door for others to think I was a push over. And that wasn't going to happen.

"I didn't hear you. Say it again." I walked toward Joe. We were now toe to toe, with a crowd around us.

"I said fuck you and fuck that fat mother..." But before Joe could finish talking, in a surprising move, Humpty nearly knocked me over to get to him.

It was one swift motion. His right hand was balled into a fist, cocked back, and unleashed in a matter of two seconds. He hit Joe dead on his chin, and I swore I heard it shatter. Joe's eyes instinctively shut tight. He stumbled and fell onto his back to a louder chorus of "Ohhs!" and "Oohs!"

From that moment, I knew we would be good friends. I didn't ask him to join me in a fight. Why would I? We barely knew each other. But the way he saw things, here stood someone challenging both he and I, and it needed to be addressed.

Sure there was going to be a fight and sure I was about to handle the issue, but he injected himself in a way he didn't have to. How many people would put themselves in a fight for someone they barely knew? So far, only one person would do such a thing and he called himself Humpty. So from that moment on, I decided to call him friend.

Joe was still on his back, wiggling in excruciating pain and I stared at Humpty who was now walking closer to the fallen leader. Humpty looked at Joe on the ground, looked at me and then said something that was probably the most profound lesson I learned up until that point in my young life.

Without blinking Humpty said, "There was too much talking. If you're gonna hit someone. Then hit him."

Chapter 10

After my late morning stroll down memory lane, I found myself back at my apartment shortly after noon. The plan was to call Humpty's family. I didn't know if they were aware of what happened. Once his body was released, I was sure they'd want to have him buried, sooner rather than later.

I've left my phone plugged in to charge for the last two days because it had been having so many problems. The most recent problem was now trying to locate it. I never charged it in the same place.

Luckily the phone rang as soon as I started looking for it. It was one of the old school rings that I remembered from my childhood house phone. No need for ring tones or fancy computer sounds. When I thought of a phone ringing, I wanted to hear a real ring.

The sound was muffled under an old newspaper, which sat atop a small bookshelf in the corner of the living room. I jotted around the coffee table and leapt at the phone before the caller was automatically sent to voicemail. It was Johnnie.

I sat on the sofa and answered the phone at the same time. "What's the deal?"

"You know my father told you not to look into that thing."

"What are you doing? Checking up on me?" I was kind of annoyed that Johnnie felt the need to even call and mention it to me. I thought he knew me better.

"I'm just saying. He told *you* not to look into it. He never said anything about me. And I've got a little information."

Information? And so soon? Deep down, I wanted to know what Johnnie was able to find out and how he came about this information, but I couldn't travel down that road.

"That's six in one hand and a half a dozen in the other. I'm hanging up now."

"Wait, wait, wait!"

At that moment there was a knock at my apartment door.

Johnnie continued. "Humpty was my boy too! I may not have known him as long or as well as you, but I'm affected by this just as you are. Now I think I know who was responsible and I'm gonna get to the bottom of this with or without you."

I swung my door open without looking through the peephole or asking who it was. That was a big mistake. With Johnnie on the phone, trying to persuade me to disobey his own father, I now had one of Metropolitan Police Department's finest standing in my doorway. It was Detective Che Aguilar.

He waited for an invitation to come inside. He received no such thing. I stood in the doorway and stared at him.

Motivated by the brief silence, Johnnie said. "Hey! Are you listening to me?"

"No. So long as you're talking that bullshit, I'm not." Without waiting for a response, I ended the call and tossed the phone on my desk. It slid up against a busted laptop that I had been meaning to get fixed. Broken phone, broken laptop, nothing seemed to be working right.

"You were supposed to come see me this morning." Aguilar said. "Can I come in?"

"How can I help you, Detective?" I asked without addressing his question. He knew he wasn't getting invited into my home.

"It's like that?"

"Yeah," I said. "It's like that."

"Well, then I'll make this quick. I'm not here about the robbery and murders that happened as a result. That's open and shut. As a matter of fact, we're not even charging the shop worker who pulled the trigger."

"That's good to know. I appreciate your coming all the way over here to tell me. Since I'm not needed, you have a nice day."

I closed my door, in an attempt to push him along his way, but Aguilar stuck his foot in the portal to prevent me from closing it completely. It's a good thing I wasn't shutting the door with force.

Aguilar pushed the door back open with his hand. "That's the thing. I never said you weren't needed. I want to talk with you about Humpty. His murder took place roughly the same time as your incident, which is where I hurried off too that night."

"I don't know anything about that." I said.

"Don't play stupid with me. You expect me to believe you didn't know what he was up to? Well let me tell you what I know. I know he was in constant communication with a mystery person all the way up until that night. I know that said mystery person was using a disposable phone. I know that people don't use disposable phones in Humpty's line of work unless they're hiding something. And finally, I know that you were the last person he called."

"You're wrong. Humpty didn't call me."

Even if everything Aguilar said was true, I wanted him to get the point. He's the police. And I don't like police. Not under any circumstance.

I've worked extremely hard to stay below the radar and out of a holding cell. But even still, they've always found ways of leaning on me in an attempt to get information about Marco. And every time they asked, they'd get the same response. *How would a restaurant host know anything about illegal activities?*

I worked hard to portray myself as a mere host at Marco's restaurant. Whether he referred to me as Jelani Jones or Anthony Ribisi, there was never concrete evidence linking me to anything illegal.

"Humpty didn't call you?" Aguilar asked. "Well, the phone company says he did. Maybe you should check your missed calls. See if you have a voicemail."

"I'll be sure to do that. Now if you don't mind."

Aguilar was crazy if he thought I would look into my call logs and voicemail while he was standing there.

"Oh. Right. I guess I'll be on my way then." But before he left, Aguilar made one last futile attempt at doing his job. "You be sure to reach out to me if you come across anything."

And with that, he was gone. From the moment he mentioned the possible call, my mind had been focused on checking. The truth is that I hadn't seen my phone in days. Humpty could have very well called me and I wouldn't know.

Sure enough, my message-waiting indicator light was blinking, alerting me to a number of unchecked voicemails. I pressed a couple of buttons to fast forward past two messages. I pressed a couple more buttons and within seconds I could hear Humpty's final words.

"Aye yo!" he started. He was so New York. I listened to the rest of his message. It served as a roadmap. Potentially pointing me directly to Humpty's killer. I was sure it was something Marco would want to hear about right away, but I needed to do a little follow up first.

I called Johnnie back.

"Have you given it some thought?" Johnnie said when he picked up.

"Answer's still the same. But I need to use your computer."

"Why?"

I looked at the pile of broken computer pieces on my desk.

"Because I can't use mine."

Chapter 11

I could tell that Johnnie was holding a grudge since I wasn't open to hearing out his idea. Whatever he had to say to me didn't matter. If it involved disobeying his father, then he was on his own. In the end, however, I wasn't going to stop him from following up on whatever he wanted to look into. I, on the other hand, had my own lead. And I needed his computer to check it out.

Johnnie leaned over my shoulder as I powered up his computer and waited for it to come on.

"It takes a minute for my computer to warm up. I guess there's no harm in talking in the meantime," he said.

"Knock yourself out."

"I have a slam dunk here, man. A friend of mine saw Humpty arguing with someone at the bar the night before he died. One of those guys you don't argue with. The type that'll see it as a disrespect and might murder your ass over it."

"I'm not listening. Better yet, share it with your old man."

"Fuck my old man!" Johnnie yelled as he retreated to the center of his living room. "You heard him. He's pulling out of the business. He's pulling *us* out of the business.

"I know this guy is gonna be at Red Lounge tonight and I have it on good fuckin' authority he knows what happened! This might be our only chance to find out the truth."

Johnnie was visibly upset. Clearly he wanted to keep the gambling houses open and thought his father's course of action was the wrong way to go. But using Humpty's murder as a way to buck against his father didn't sit well with me.

Thank God the computer hummed on before he continued his tirade. I wasn't in the mood to hear him bitch and moan about it anyway. I pulled up the internet browser and made my way to Gmail.

"Don't you wanna know?" Johnnie pleaded.

I didn't bother answering him. I stared at the screen and typed in a username and password that hadn't been used in over six months. It was a special email account, used for transmitting videos that only Humpty and I were aware of. It was our own little secret.

The inbox was barren with the exception of one email that was dated the night Humpty was killed. This concerned me. The process was to open emails, watch the videos, and then immediately delete emails. The last time I accessed this account, I was sure to delete everything. It should have been empty.

I opened the email, clicked on the attachment and a video began playing. Johnnie walked up to get a better look.

"What's that?"

"Let's just look first and see."

The quality of the video wasn't the best, but it was good enough for us to make out Humpty standing outside of the Verizon Center. The video camera was across the street from him. Next we saw a taller man walk toward him, away from the camera, and hold a brief conversation with our friend.

The next thing we saw made me furious. The unknown man pulled out what looked like a machete and without warning sliced into Humpty. And then it was over. He disappeared into the crowd.

"What the hell!" Johnnie shouted. "How'd the hell did you get that video?"

"It's a precautionary system I put in place years ago," I said, still staring at the screen.

"Precautionary system?"

I hit the replay button on the video to watch it again. I needed to look at everything about the recording.

"Only when I had meetings set. None of the other organizations were kind on doing work with a young black man. Coming to a meeting and finding me instead of some Italian named Anthony presented certain challenges."

"How does the video play into it?"

"This was my backup plan. Just in case they wanted to get creative. Let's say the meeting didn't go as planned. It was proof I did my part. Worst case scenario, let's say it was a setup and I didn't make it out. Everything would have been recorded."

After watching the video one last time, I felt my anger growing more and more. I had watched it enough. I logged out of the email account and turned to face Johnnie.

"I'd always get to the meeting location a few hours ahead of time. I'd set the camera up where it wouldn't be seen. Then I leave and come back when it was time to work. If anything happened to me and I couldn't retrieve the camera, a video file was wirelessly emailed to the account I just checked. And if Humpty didn't hear from me that night, he knew to check the account the following day."

My plan was to always make sure that the whole story was told, even if I wasn't around to tell it. Humpty clearly made the same plans the night he was killed.

Now I was in a position I hadn't been in earlier. The pain of Humpty's murder walked hand in hand with the anger that came from watching it three times. In living color. I wanted whoever was responsible to pay. But in order to ensure retribution I had to do something I had never done in my life, disobey Marco.

"So when do you want to show the video to my father?" Johnnie asked.

The question hung like a helium balloon, loosing air. It was like a challenge to an anger-fueled warrior looking to avenge the death of a fallen loved one. I knew my next words would set in motion a course of action that I wouldn't be able to reverse. I knew it. But I said them anyway.

"Tomorrow." I said. "But tonight, I feel like getting a drink. Let's hit up Red Lounge."

Chapter 12

Johnnie and I decided to make a visit to Red Lounge around ten o'clock, so I could take care of something else first. It was nearly time for him to pick me up.

I knew I had to call Humpty's mother, but I didn't want to. Here I was, sitting on the front steps of my apartment, with the intention of comforting her and there she was, comforting me.

Humpty's mother was a strong woman. She was raised on the island of Jamaica and migrated to Bronx, by herself, in her early twenties. By that time, she had given birth to her only son and they shared a tiny one-bedroom apartment on 235th Street and White Plains Road.

She worked hard to support her child. When he was old enough to stay home at night, she worked the overnight shift at a twenty-four hour diner in order to pay for nursing school during the day. And once she graduated from school, it was fulltime nursing from then on.

This wasn't the stereotypical story of the Jamaican who worked "tree" jobs. She was focused on a particular goal and achieved it. This unwavering determination must have been genetically passed on to Humpty.

After having gained a year's worth of experience, his mother applied for a position at George Washington Hospital. It was a smart move for her. The salary was better and the cost of living in Washington, DC, at the time, was less expensive than New York. She worked, raised her son, and saved her money.

When the time came for her to move again, she did. In her mind, her son had grown to become a man and she gave him a choice. He could've stayed in DC or relocated with his mother to Orlando, FL. Humpty decided to stay. His mother now regretted having given him the option.

We were getting off the phone as I noticed Coco walking down the block from her parked car.

"Mi luv yuh too, mumma," I said before hanging up the phone.

"Humpty's mother?" Coco asked. "I heard about it a couple hours ago. I can always tell when you're talking to her. You go into what little patois you know."

I got the feeling Coco could also tell I was a little on edge. She spun around to sit down next to me. Since she knew about the murder, I knew the purpose of her visit. She had always been a great friend to me.

"Thanks for coming to check on me," I said.

She placed her head on my shoulder and threaded her arm through mine.

"No need to thank me."

"I'm about to leave though."

"Really? Where to?"

I debated on whether or not to tell her. There was a noticeable hesitation on my part, which created an awkward silence.

"Where to, sir?"

"I'd rather not say."

Coco rolled her eyes and let out a long sigh. Just then Johnnie's candy apple red Camaro came to a screeching halt in front of my building and he honked his horn.

"Fine then, don't tell me!" Coco said as I got up. "But I'm going to be right here until you get back."

"That's your choice. You have a perfectly good car up a half a block."

"Let's go!" Johnnie yelled from his car.

"Don't be an ass, Jelani," Coco said.

"Don't sit out here all night," I replied, hopping into Johnnie's candy apple.

"Are you ready to handle this?" He asked.

I looked at Johnnie as if a reply was unnecessary. I was sitting in his car. I was ready. Probably more ready than him. He pulled off but before we made it halfway down the street, I could see Coco in front of my building. The look on her face made it clear she wasn't happy.

"Wait!" I said.

I groaned and grabbed the handle of the car door. Jumping out of the vehicle, I made my way back to Coco.

"Oh come on man!" Johnnie yelled at me.

I ran back to Coco and placed a set of keys in her hand.

"Go upstairs, please. I'll be back soon."

Coco didn't say anything in return. She took her time making her way to the front door. I watched as she walked into the building. I loved watching her walk. It was a work of art.

By the time I made it back to the car, Johnnie was standing outside of the driver's side with his arm resting on the roof. "Now are you ready?"

Chapter 13

Coco had been inside Jelani's apartment before, but this was her first time alone. When she walked in, her first instinct was to head to the sofa and turn on the television. She did, in fact, turn on the television. But instead of sitting down, she decided to take a look around.

Since Jelani was such a secret squirrel about many of the things in his life, she felt this was a prime opportunity to do a little snooping. Perhaps learn a little more about the friend that she knew so little about and maybe find a clue to who Anthony Ribisi was.

As a therapist, being invasive was a part of her job. But that was with willing participants. Coco understood there was a difference between what she did in her office with clients and what she was doing in her friend's apartment.

Jelani hadn't asked her to look through his photos in an attempt at pulling together different phases of his life, but she was doing it anyway. She didn't get permission to open desk drawers and look under his bed for a diary or journal that might shed light on his thoughts. But "*so what,*" she thought. She was on her knees regardless.

It was easy for her to rationalize this invasion of his privacy. If he were forthcoming about his life, then it wouldn't be necessary. And it brought her some accomplished satisfaction. His photographs for instance.

There were four pictures that caught her attention and two of them were of his mother. This told her that even with the present negative feelings he had about their relationship, he still held a special place in his heart for her. To Coco, this meant there was a chance for reconciliation. She promised herself that she would try to facilitate that reconciliation whenever the opportunity presented itself.

The other two pictures were of Jelani as a young boy, roughly five years old. She hadn't noticed them before. What interested her most was that there was another young boy in the picture and it wasn't Humpty. These were pictures from well before the two of them met.

After visually comparing the complexion, skin and hair texture, and facial similarities between boys and the picture of Jelani's mother, the only conclusion Coco could come to was that the boys were related. They were brothers probably, maybe a year apart. Jelani had a brother and Coco had no idea.

Her snooping paid off in that respect. It served as positive reinforcement for her to continue. And so she did. After looking under the bed, she walked into the bathroom. Then she went into the kitchen. Then she looked around the living room again. Ultimately walking back into the bedroom. She hadn't looked in his closet.

It wasn't a large closet but he had it organized pretty well. Dress slacks and shirts on hangers. He had a few suits. And there were sweaters folded on an upper shelf. The shoes and sneakers were organized on the floor of the closet as well. And then she saw it.

This snooping thing wasn't new to her. Even as a teenager she was inquisitive. While in relationships, boyfriends would leave their unlocked phones around her at their own risk. Her friends told her to stop being so nosey. They warned that sooner or later she would find something she didn't want to see. Which is exactly happened in Jelani's closet.

Deep into his closet, behind the second row of shoes, she found what looked to be a briefcase. She pulled the bulky object out only to find it was much larger than a briefcase but smaller than a suitcase.

The black hardshell case was square in shape. Coco noticed that the latches weren't locked. She laid the case down flat and lifted up the top. She found the inside of the case was filled with black foam and contained two hollowed out spaces...each for a handgun.

One of the handguns was missing.

Chapter 14

Red Lounge was more of a hole-in-the-wall dive bar than like the ultra sophisticated nightclubs that sprung up in the neighborhood. It was at the intersection of Fourteenth and U Streets. Exactly two blocks away and around the corner from the restaurant.

This made it a convenient place for me to grab a quick drink after work. I made it a point to never drink while working a shift. Red Lounge, however, was a different story. I was a regular.

The owners were an older Moroccan couple. They bought the building when real estate was dirt cheat in the area and transformed its two floors into something respectable. And what I liked about it most was that it was low-key.

Over the years, the lounge got a reputation for having one of the better DJs in the city. It wasn't a pretty place, but if you wanted to dance your butt off, it was the place to be. Partiers would spend their happy hours at the chic establishments up and down U Street, then come to Red Lounge for late night dancing and sweat out their hair.

Johnnie and I approached the entrance of the lounge. Before I could get to the front door, Johnnie grabbed me by the arm.

"Shit man! I can't go in there."

"Why not?" I asked.

"The bouncer is patting down at the door." He pulled me closer to whisper, "And I'm packing."

I nodded in the direction of the car. Johnnie got the message.

"Fuck!" He exclaimed as he jogged back to the car to hide his gun.

When he returned we walked past the line that was forming to the left of the front door. We were waved over as soon as the bouncer saw us. I had already made eye contact with him when Johnnie went back to the car.

His name was Smitty and he was built like a linebacker. He looked like one too. He was the spitting image of Lawrence Taylor from the New York Giants, so I called him LT every once and awhile.

Because of his size and background, bouncing at the club was a perfect gig for him. This whale of a man used to be a detective for the Metropolitan Police Department.

After ten years of service, he abruptly resigned. No one knew why. Well, Marco knew. But he would never share details. He would only tell me to be mindful of whom I called a partner. He would always tell me that Smitty learned a tough lesson on loyalty the hard way.

Smitty loved him some Marco Ribisi. When everyone avoided him like Typhoid Mary, Marco helped him with money initially and then by lining up jobs to keep him on his feet. And every once and awhile, Smitty still took jobs from Marco.

Smitty gave me the fake pat down that he did every week. Sometimes, two or three times a week. He never put real energy into searching people he knew and their guests.

"Fatimah and Raz here tonight?" I asked walking in. They were the owners of the lounge.

"Raz isn't here yet. Fatimah is behind the bar."

That was good news. Even though she never gave me free drinks, she always poured with a heavy hand. It was like getting three drinks for the price of one.

Johnnie and I made a beeline to Fatimah. She already had a Makers on the rocks waiting for me. I threw up two fingers and she poured another for Johnnie. He was too busy looking around the lounge to notice.

"So who are we looking for?" I asked as I passed him his drink.

"Marty Fucker," he said over his shoulder.

I coughed out my drink and shot Johnnie the look of a thousand deaths."Shit man! You never said it was Marty Fucker!"

Martin Fauconier. Marty Fucker, for short. He was an upper level protector for the Gianni Oronzio crime family. The curly haired blonde was the product of a French mother and Italian father, and he was known in the streets as the Hatchet.

As it goes, hatchets were his weapons of choice for up close kills. The urban legend was that he carried two hatchets on him at all times. But no one who has had a confrontation with him lived to talk about it. This was a fact. Another fact...Marty Fucker was dangerous.

"There he is." Johnnie said. He spied Marty sitting against the wall in a semi-private area of the lounge. "I'm going over."

"To say what?" Mocking Johnnie, I intoned, "Hey Hatchet. Can I talk to you? I think you killed one of my friends."

The night just became unpredictably dangerous and we needed to leave. Immediately.

In an attempt at reasoning with Johnnie, I said, "Let's forget this, for now. We take this to your father in the morning. Let him deal with it from the top down."

But there was nothing I could tell Johnnie. He was intent on approaching Marty. Hatchets or not, it felt as if Johnnie wanted to prove a point.

And there was no way I could leave him. How would I explain to Marco that his son was hacked into little pieces because I left him alone at the club with Marty Fucker?

"Johnnie. Let's think about it. There's gotta be a better..." And before I could finish my sentence, he was walking over.

"Hey Marty!" Johnnie yelled over the music.

Marty was sitting between two knockouts. One was a white girl and the other was Latina. I recognized the white girl as a dancer from the Washington Wizards cheerleading team. She seemed to recognize me as well. I dated her dance captain earlier in the year and we all partied from time to time. The other beauty was a stranger to me.

Johnnie got to within five feet of Marty when out of nowhere three gigantic bodyguards grabbed him by his collar and began pushing him backwards.

"Marty is busy right now," one of the behemoths said.

"Yeah. Make an appointment," said another.

"Get the fuck off me!" Johnnie squirmed in the giants' grasp.

I made my way over toward the commotion before Smitty could notice and would have to address it.

"It's all good, gentleman. We're on our way."

Before I could grab Johnnie and turn to walk away, Marty looked up from his company and saw Johnnie and flicked a glance at me.

"Hey! Ribisi!" he shouted with an intoxicated slur. "Come over here!"

Johnnie looked at me as to say, "Put your big boy pants on and let's go!"

He brushed past the bodyguards and stood in front of Marty and his two guests.

"Sorry about the scuffle. Sit down. How's the old man?"

"Nah. I'm good. I just wanted to ask you something."

"Sit down," Marty insisted again, sounding more sober than the first time he spoke.

Johnnie pulled a chair from an adjoining area and reluctantly sat. I remained standing. Marty took that time to light a cigarette.

"So, what do you want to know?" Marty asked.

"Well, an incident took place the other night and I wanted to know if you could shed light on it."

Marty whispered to the young female companions. I couldn't hear what he said, but each left us and walked over to the bar. No one was in our immediate vicinity, other than the bodyguards. Marty looked me over.

"You're Anthony? Aren't you? I haven't met you yet." He got up from his seat and walked over to me with his hand extended. While we shook hands Marty pulled me in closer and said, "I've heard so much about you. You might even consider me a fan of your work.

"You and I are a lot alike, you know? From what I've been told, you're really proficient. And it's almost passion-fueled. But I'm not sure if you understand that this is as far as we'll go. Me, not being fully Italian, and all. And hell, you! You're nowhere near Italian. There's a glass ceiling for us, my friend."

Marty intentionally ignored Johnnie all together and couldn't care less about what he just asked. Being blown off visibly aggravated him. Johnnie shot out of his seat like a cannon.

He grabbed at Marty's shoulders to spin him around and get his attention.

"Look here, Marty!"

Before he could finish another word, he was tackled into the wall and held there by two of Marty's bodyguards. He was unable to move.

Marty looked at Johnnie, sucked his teeth and shook his head from side to side.

"You need to be more careful of the company you keep, Anthony. Hotheads tend to get the cooler heads fucked up. There's a reason I'm called Marty *Fucker,* you know."

Marty stepped past the third bodyguard standing behind me, to make his way to the young ladies at the bar.

"Now if you'll excuse me boys. I have a couple things I need to get into tonight."

Marty nodded at his personal security. "Fellas." And then Marty quickly exited the building with the girls.

I knew what that head nod meant. Whether inside the lounge or out in the back alley, Marty was making it clear that he wanted his security to at least rough us up, and at worst, put our lifeless bodies in the trunk of a car.

And I didn't have the patience to find out.

Just then, a waiter was walking past with an unopened bottle of Moet on a platter for some wannabe baller who ordered bottle service. Before anyone could react, I grabbed the bottle and swung it violently at the head of the bouncer closest to me. Goliath hit the deck. But he wasn't down for the count.

Pandemonium broke out once everyone saw me hop onto the burly bodyguard and continue my attack with the bottle. Following my lead, and out of self-preservation, Johnnie began to wildly swing at one of the two bodyguards who were now looking at me in shock.

He was able to connect to the chin of the largest bodyguard but within seconds the last bodyguard knocked him to the floor. It was now two against one in his corner.

I saw Smitty trying to fight against the current of the crowd rushing out of the door. But he had no luck. Everyone was running out, pushing him away. At least if he could have made his way in, that would have evened the odds. There was no way Smitty would have swung on Johnnie or me.

Satisfied that Goliath wouldn't get up from the floor anytime soon, I ran over to Johnnie who had assumed the fetal position in order to protect his head and neck. He was in the process of being stomped, damn near into the floor. So I did the only thing that I could think to do.

I pulled a black 9mm Glock from my waistband and shot a slug into the floor. I chambered another round, pointed at the head of the closest bodyguard, and yelled loud enough to be heard over the music that was still playing.

"ENOUGH!"

Chapter 15

Marco and Nick Nick walked into Red Lounge like they owned the place. They walked straight to Raz's office, which was past the bar. Fatimah smiled at them, wiping down bar top.

Smitty stood guard at the door to make sure no one came in or out. But I think it was mostly to keep us in our places until Marco arrived.

Raz rushed into his office three steps after Marco and Nick Nick. "Oh my God! I'm so sorry about this Mr. Ribisi. I was up in Baltimore and came down as soon as I got the call."

Raz knew what type of weight Marco pulled. He apologized out of respect, or maybe it was fear.

"No need. None of this is your fault," Marco said. He looked at me and to Johnnie with a longer gaze. "But could you give us the room?"

"By all means." Raz left us alone, pulling Smitty along with him.

Marco walked around to the empty chair at Raz's desk and sat down. He spun the chair from side to side, testing its oscillation. Once in a comfortable position, he settled in as if it was his desk back at the restaurant.

"What did I say?"

It was silent. So much that if a feather fell from the ceiling, you could hear the air being split.

"I know what I said. Do you two know what I said?" He looked at Nick Nick. "Nick! You heard what I said, right?"

"I sure did." Nick Nick said, lighting a cigarette.

"Ok, great. So we know I was talking loud enough to be heard."

"You don't have to talk to us like we children," Johnnie interrupted, barely above a mumble.

"Obviously I do!" Marco shot back. "You two have no idea what you've done!"

"It's my fault, Marco," I interjected. "I shouldn't have let us come down here, and then I let it get out of hand."

Not in the mood to back down, Johnnie said, "What are talking about? You don't have to apologize! We had good reason and we acted on it."

"No!" Marco slapped his hand down on the desk with a force that nearly split the desktop in two. Everything on the desk jumped in the air. "You're shooting into the dark and jeopardizing everything that I'm trying to do!"

"I've had enough of this!" Johnnie said, standing to his feet. "Tell him, Anthony! Tell him about the video!"

Marco turned his attention on me. "What video?" he asked.

Sensing that Marco wasn't in the most pleasant of moods, I weighed my words carefully. I didn't think it was wise to tell Marco I recorded almost every meeting I had on his behalf. Even though all the videos were ultimately deleted, I'm sure he still wouldn't have been happy with that action.

"Humpty set up a surveillance camera for observation the night he was murdered."

I told them that a video was wirelessly emailed to me and filled them in on the details of the night.

"He was setup, without a doubt. He wasn't mugged and it wasn't an accident," Johnnie said. "I looked into it and got a name. Marty Fucker. You said yourself, not to do anything because we didn't know for sure what happen. Well, now we do."

"Once you came into this information, what should you have done with it?" Marco asked. "Anthony? What should you have done?"

"We should have come you."

"Bingo. And now, I have to clean up your mess."

"What mess, Pop?" Johnnie said.

"There are things happening here, you know nothing about," Marco said.

Johnnie walked to the door leading out of the office. "Really? Sounds to me like you're just scared. More concerned with getting rid of everything you built over the years. And for what? A damn restaurant."

Johnnie walked out the office to insure he had the final word. Marco looked at Nick Nick; they rarely spoke a word to each other. But they'd been together so long, they could read each other's thoughts.

Nick Nick followed after Johnnie. This left Marco and I alone.

"Do you remember when you first came to our restaurant?" It was a rhetorical question. He had no intention of waiting for an answer. "You were a young boy then and far too young to work. Well at least legally."

Marco walked from around the desk and sat on the edge, next to where I was standing.

"You were tired of bagging groceries at the neighborhood supermarket." Marco laughed to himself. "It didn't pay enough money, you said. You remember that?"

"Yeah. I remember. You hired me to wipe tables and sweep the floor."

"And a week later you came into the restaurant piping hot mad and ready to fight. One of the boys was out front teasing you because he thought you had been begging us for food. And your pride wasn't having it. You worked for your money and if you walked out with some food as an added benefit, then it was what it was.

"You ran straight to my office and grabbed Johnnie's baseball bat. I pulled you close, and do you remember what I said to you?"

I thought for a minute and said, "What are you doing? You're gonna get blood on a perfectly good bat."

"No, the other thing!" Marco said.

"Yeah. I remember. There are only two types of battles."

"The unnecessary battle," Marco said.

"And the unavoidable battle," I said.

"Exactly. It's simple. Johnnie's upset over Humpty, but this was unnecessary."

"You know good and well that's not what's really upsetting Johnnie."

Marco sighed and looked to the floor. "My son is upset because he thinks I don't want him to run the family business. Which he thinks is the real reason why I'm closing the houses. He thinks I don't trust him to be a good successor."

Marco started walking toward the door.

"Come on. Let's get out of here," Marco said. "I have a meeting tomorrow to straighten all of this out."

Marco stopped short before exiting the office. "Let me ask you a question. If you had to trust Johnnie to run the business in my absence, would you?"

Marco knew he was putting me on the spot. What happened tonight wasn't an isolated incident. It was Johnnie's modus operandi. Flawed action based on hotheaded decisions.

All I could do was stare at Marco. I couldn't say that I'd be completely comfortable with Johnnie in control. I didn't want to say it. So I didn't say a word.

"You're kinda quiet." Marco nodded. "That's what I thought. Don't worry, Anthony. I know what I'm doing."

Chapter 16

I didn't get home until well after three in the morning. If Coco was awake, I would have been shocked. To be honest, I would be surprised if she was at my place at all. I let out a sigh of relief when I saw her purse on my coffee table.

First thing I did was walk in the kitchen and pour a glass of water. In the drawer next to the sink, I found a bottle of aspirin. I grabbed the bottle and replaced it with the gun from my waistband.

My hand was beginning to hurt from the fight. I took the aspirin and water into the living room and sat on the sofa, where I downed the drink and three tablets in one gulp.

So as not to wake Coco, I got up and gingerly walked to the bathroom. Even if I didn't shower at the end of the day, I would always brush my teeth. I turned the water on to a low stream and brushed as quietly as I could.

I didn't want to wake the girl but I had a burning feeling to set my eyes on her. I still hadn't forgotten the kiss from the other night. The thought of us possibly developing our friendship into something more made me feel like I had a little high school crush. It was a fresh feeling that I hadn't felt in a long time.

I peeked into the bedroom just to look at her. It felt natural for me to want to make sure she was comfortable. I could hear the deep breaths she took while she laid on her side. The next minute, I found myself standing over her.

Without thinking, I leaned over and gently gave her a kiss on her cheek and then another on her forehead. She shifted slightly, but remained asleep. Her deep breaths weren't interrupted.

Feeling very stalkerish, I forced myself to go back into the living room. I was certain climbing in the bed would wake her. The sofa would provide a comfortable enough substitute to the bed.

I was laid out and exhausted. But I couldn't go to sleep. The thought of Coco in my bed had my mind racing. I wanted to be close to her. I wanted to feel her body next to mine. Maybe even accidentally brush the back of my hand against her breasts in the middle of the night. I imagined myself spooning her so I could wrap her within my hold.

My eyelids were starting to hang heavy. After the day I had, sleep was sorely needed. Maybe I'd have a peaceful sleep and dream of her. I deliberately thought of Coco in the hopes that I would see her in my dreams. My eyelids were shut and I felt my own breathing become long and deep.

Before I fell completely into REM sleep, even with closed eyes, I could hear the shuffle of soft steps moving closer. I felt a body lie down in front of mine. She took my arm and pulled it around her waist, and intentionally cupped one of my hands over her breast.

The last thing I felt before falling into a coma-like sleep was Coco's other hand run across my freshly scraped knuckles. She dipped her head and kissed my swollen hand.

Then we slept.

Chapter 17

"Marco!" Gianni Oronzio exclaimed with his lengthy arms held wide, walking into the office. He was escorted by Nick Nick. Marco stood to greet him, returning the smile knowing it didn't match the tone of their meeting.

The two men greeted each other with a warm embrace and kisses to each side of the face before they sat down. Nick Nick stood by the door like a sentinel on guard.

"This misunderstanding, Marco, it's not good. Marty feels like your son crossed the line. One of his security personnel had to get his jaw wired."

"Really. What a shame." Marco's mono-toned disinterest was apparent. He didn't want to hear about one of Oronzio's worker's worker. Marco was focused on more important things. "Forgive me for not appearing overly concerned. You know what I want to talk about."

"Ahh. That's right. Straight to the point. I always liked that about you," Oronzio replied.

"Here's the deal. You can report to the other bosses that the decision's been made. The last gambling house was shut down a month ago. They'll be no more activities in that arena and from now on, my business will be this here restaurant."

"Marco, do you see how that could make the other bosses nervous? I don't know if anyone ever deployed the exit strategy you're suggesting. In the past, people have walked away, and it's always been dangerously complicated. Are you sure you don't want to reconsider?"

"I'm walking away, Gianni. And there's nothing anyone can do about it. Look at it like this: underground gambling is up for grabs in the District of Columbia. Maybe you might want it."

Oronzio let out a laugh. "Maybe."

"Good. Then it's settled."

"Not so fast. I have to bring it back to the bosses at the next meeting."

"You were supposed to have already done that." Marco's eyes narrowed.

"Yes. And we did. Everyone gave you the benefit of the doubt. They like you because you've always been faithful. But there were still some concerns. And this latest business with your son...It changes things."

"My son has nothing to do with this."

"Who knows? He seems to be on a warpath. Thinking Marty had something to do with those hits. Come on man. Marty doing that would reflect poorly on me. Your son has to understand this before moving forward."

"Well, I don't control how my son thinks."

"Or what he does?" Oronzio asked. "Then we might have a problem."

Marco stood from his desk. There was nothing more to say. Oronzio was playing hardball, when the matter should have been softball, all the way. "Ok. Well, you go and talk with them. Let me know where everyone stands."

Oronzio stood too. "Will do. I mean...I've got people I need to answer to."

Marco knew that was bullshit.

"I'll talk with Johnnie," Marco said.

"Great. And let him know, I thought Humpty was a good kid. Anthony I've only met once. I liked him. We don't have any problem with your people, Marco."

"I look forward to hearing back from you." Marco shook hands with Oronzio. "Nick Nick. Make sure Gianni makes it out ok."

Nick Nick stepped up to escort Oronzio out of the restaurant. While he was gone, Marco was bothered by something that was said.

He picked up the phone and called for Jelani. "Get in here, Anthony. I think we have a bigger problem."

* * *

I walked into Marco's office along with Nick Nick. Marco was pacing the floor. That meant he was in thought.

"Nick Nick. You heard him too, right?"

"I certainly did." Nick Nick replied.

I wanted to wait a second before asking questions. Give the grown folks some time to include the child into the discussion.

"He must think I'm stupid," Marco said, shaking his head at the floor. It looked as if he was growing angrier by the moment.

"We can't ignore the obvious. He could have let it slip on purpose," Nick Nick said.

"I don't think he did. Don't give Gianni Oronzio that much credit. Tact isn't a strong suit of his. He's as dumb as a bull in a suit."

The two of them finally decided to acknowledge my presence.

"How did Johnnie know to go looking for Marty?" Marco asked me.

"I think he got the lead from a friend of his."

"I want you to find this friend of his and bring him here. You can take Johnnie, but let me make this clear, I want him brought to me."

"Will do," I said. "But is someone going to tell me what's happening?"

"I'm starting to lean toward your idea that Marty had a hand in Humpty's murder now," Marco said.

No shit, I thought. I'd never say that to Marco aloud. But Johnnie and I were already sold on that line of thinking.

"Do you wanna tell him the rest?" Nick Nick asked.

"The rest of what? There's more?" I questioned.

"I'm almost certain there was another hit attempted." Marco shifted his eyes to Nick Nick.

"Oh yeah? On who?"

Both Marco and Nick Nick turned their heads and looked at me.

"On you," Marco said.

I let out a slight laugh. There's no way the two of them were serious. There had been no attempt on my life and I told them that.

"Sorry, guys. No machete wielding maniac tried to cut out my intestines."

"You're absolutely right," Nick Nick said.

Then Marco added, "But you were in the middle of a robbery that very same night. One I suspect should have ended with you pumped full of bullets, had it not been for a quick thinking cashier."

Nick Nick put his hand on my shoulder and said, "Trust us, son. Those guys weren't there to rob the place. They were there to kill you. Two hits. One night."

Chapter 18

I wanted to talk with Johnnie before showing up to his apartment, but my phone had lost all of its power again. So showing up, unannounced, was the easiest thing to do.

Even though we hadn't spoken, I knew he'd be home. After the fallout from the Red Lounge confrontation, Johnnie went missing. And for him, missing usually meant he locked himself in his apartment. Or better yet, locked the rest of the world out.

I knocked on the front door to get Johnnie's attention. After the third time, it was clear he had no intention of answering.

"Johnnie!" I yelled.

I pressed my ear against the door. It was silent. But Johnnie wasn't fooling anyone. I knew he was inside. His car was parked out front. And I knew what needed to be said for him to open the door. It was childish, but it needed to be done.

"You were right, Johnnie," I spoke into the door. "Your father sent me to get you. We need to talk to your guy. So open up, and let's get to work."

I backed up and leaned against the wall. I waited through the sound of locks turning. And sure enough, I heard the slide of a deadbolt and then a chain lock. Telling Johnnie he was right was the same as saying *Open Sesame*.

"So now he wants to listen to me?" Johnnie asked.

He looked ready for bed, wearing a pair of basketball shorts and a wife beater. He even had a toothbrush hanging from the corner of his mouth.

I didn't feel the need to burst his bubble, so I kept my answer simple.

"Yes sir." His grimace turned into a crocked smile. A look of gratification washed over his face. "So get dressed. We've got to go."

"I'll be right back." He ran into the bathroom to spit out toothpaste.

I could hear him shuffling between the bathroom and bedroom. Dresser drawers were being open and shut. He emerged from the bedroom, fully clothed. There was a new sense of excitement on his part. His earlier action had been validated and it looked like he was ready to step up for the family. At least that's what I thought.

"What are you doing?" Johnnie asked as he walked back into the living room.

While he was running around, I had taken it upon myself to get on his computer. I hadn't deleted the video file or the email from earlier. And it was a good thing.

"I only want another look. Something about it had been bothering me since we first watched it."

"Something other than the murder, you mean?"

I paid Johnnie no mind. I was busy looking at the movements the killer made over Humpty's body.

"Yup. That's what I thought." I pointed to the computer screen. "See how he lifted the pants leg?"

"And he's digging something out of the boot. What do you think it is?"

"Well, this was an exchange of some service or goods for money, right? Humpty's voicemail said he had some info he was being paid for. I really can't see what it is, but my guess is that it's a flash drive of some kind."

If my assumption was correct, then I was almost certain that the information was still sitting on Humpty's computer. We needed to know what was so important that Oronzio felt the need to kill for it.

"Call your boy. Tell him we're making a pit stop, and then we're coming to get him. We need go to Humpty's first."

"Ok. Let me get Vinnie's number."

"Vinnie who?" I asked. Praying it wasn't Skinny Vinnie from Southeast. Everyone called him Skinny Vinnie because he was as skinny as a floor lamp.

Before Johnnie could answer me, he was already on the phone with him.

"Hey Skinny! We're on our way to get you. Hold tight, man." Johnnie was silent for a minute. He looked at me in disbelief and said, "He's not trying to connect with us."

Johnnie looked at me and shook his head in desperation. Thoroughly annoyed, I snatched his phone. It sounded like Skinny Vinnie was crying on the other end.

"I can't do this anymore," was the first thing he said. "You guys gonna have to figure this shit out on your own. They following me, man. They following me!"

"Relax, Vinnie. It's Anthony. I want you to stay there. I need to make one stop and then I'm coming to get you."

"I don't have time to wait. They've been on my ass all day."

"It'll be all right. Lock your doors and don't move. I'll be there soon. I promise."

Vinnie was quiet for what seemed like an eternity. Then he said, "Ok. Anthony. You got an hour and a half. There's a bus leaving town with my name on it. If you don't get me by then, I'm gone."

It would only take fifteen minutes to get to Humpty's and maybe another thirty at most to go through his computer and find what we needed. That would leave more than enough time to grab Vinnie. So I agreed and hung up.

"You must be crazy!" I said to Johnnie. "All of this because of what Skinny Vinnie from Southeast told you? Are you crazy?"

"What?" Johnnie responded. He was oblivious.

"You're father is expecting us to bring this guy back to him, so we have to. But Skinny Vinnie is notoriously known for his affinity for Love Boat."

"He likes watching old television shows, so what?"

"Television shows?" I wish Johnnie had been joking but he wasn't. He knew nothing about Boat. "It's a hallucinogen, you dickhead!"

So here we were, about to go to war over the word of an addict whose drug of choice made him see things that didn't really exist. Who knew Johnnie was that clueless?

"Love Boat, huh?" Johnnie asked. "Really?"

Chapter 19

The Adams Morgan neighborhood Humpty lived in was buzzing with its usual nighttime activity. Outside of the building, horns were honking, music blasting and a slur of loud and drunken conversation spiking and fading.

In an era where a watered down vodka and cranberry cost fifteen bucks at fancy bars, Adams Morgan was extremely popular with the college crowd. It was littered with the cost effective hole in the wall alternatives, offering two-dollar drinks and jumbo pizza slices. It was a college students' dream.

Humpty's seven-story building didn't have an elevator, so Johnnie and I jogged up to the sixth floor and made our way to the end of the long darkened hallway. The apartment we wanted was on the left. The only light that worked in the hallway was above Humpty's door.

He made it a habit of replacing that particular bulb whenever it was out. He liked to be able to see who was standing outside his door.

Johnnie grabbed the doorknob and twisted it back and forth. "How are we getting in?"

Johnnie dropped down to one knee and took a closer look at the keyhole. "I heard you was pretty good at picking a lock. You're gonna have to show me how to do that."

While Johnnie was preoccupied with the door, I turned around and looked for the fire extinguisher compartment encased in the wall opposite of Humpty's door. I opened the small door and removed the fire extinguisher.

"Wait a minute. You sure you wanna break this door down? Would it be easier to just pick the lock and not draw attention to us?"

I placed the extinguisher on the floor and then felt along the ceiling on the compartment. And just as I thought, it was there. I carefully pealed down a strip of black electrical tape. I turned around and showed Johnnie why there wasn't a need to pick a lock. Humpty's spare key was on the other side of the tape.

"Ok," Johnnie said. "That's just as good."

I felt uneasy walking into Humpty's apartment. I thought about the many times we sat on the sofa and watched the Wizards or Redskins games. There were plenty of parties and shindigs hosted at his home. Food, fun, and alcohol. And for the first time, I was confronting the reality that those days would never happen again.

My friend was gone. But I had to stay focused because time was ticking and I was in search of something. Exactly what, I didn't know. But I was hoping that I'd know it once I saw it.

There was a computer on the desk, adjacent to the sofa and a laptop on the coffee table. I grabbed the open laptop that faced the sofa and asked Johnnie to boot up the desktop.

While the login screen of the laptop was already glowing and requesting a password, Johnnie appeared frustrated when his login screen came to life.

"Shit! It's password protected."

"Calm down," I said. "Type in 'banana pudding,' all in lower case."

"Space or no space?"

"Use the space. Hump used the same password for every computer he's ever had."

"Let me guess. He was a fan of the desert?"

"To be honest, I don't know. I never saw him eat the thing."

Now that both computers were humming and ready to go, we started looking through every folder we could find. We worked quickly because we knew we were up against a deadline to get Skinny Vinnie. I started with folders on the *Desktop*, then moved to folders in the *Documents* file, and then made my way to folders in the *Downloads* file.

It had taken us a little longer to go through Humpty's computer than I thought and we were coming up empty. Just as I was about to try my luck in the *Trash Bin* to see what had been deleted, I felt something that caught my attention. It was a cool breeze on the back on my neck.

The breeze meant that the window behind me was open. This struck me as weird for one reason; Humpty never opened his windows. And when I say never, I really mean *never*. There were two things that Humpty hated about his seven-floor walk up. First, living on the sixth floor without an elevator and second, not having window screens.

As big and as threatening as Humpty was, for whatever reason, he became very unsettled around bugs. The thought of them crawling on his skin would render him catatonic. So living in a building without window screens, simply meant that he'd never open the windows. He had central air-conditioning, so in the summer, he didn't care.

But here, his window was opened. Allowing the cool night air to breeze into his apartment. And the window wasn't cracked. It was wide open. As Johnnie continued his computer search, I turned around and faced the window that was immediately behind me. I leaned out and looked down, past the fire escape, to the alley below. I also reached my head around and looked up the fire escape toward the roof, which was only one story above us.

I pulled my body back into the apartment, shutting the window with a loud thump. Sitting back down, I stared at the laptop screen and then looked at the computer Johnnie clicked away on.

"Someone was here."

"What do mean?" Johnnie asked without looking away from his computer.

"Exactly what I said. This window shouldn't be open." I stood from the sofa and paced the living room floor to get my blood flowing and give some thought to the different possibilities. "They probably came down from the roof. Man, we might not find anything on these computers."

"Relax. No one was here."

"Like I said, this window should NOT be open. Hump doesn't open his windows. Not for anything. Something's not right here. And these computers?"

"What about the computers? I've been rummaging through this thing for nearly thirty minutes, so it's not like they've been wiped clean."

"Maybe not. But the desktop computer was powered down and the laptop was alive and waiting for us, like it had just been turned on. Think about it. What if someone got here before we did, heard us in the hallway and then made their way out the window?"

"I don't know." Johnnie said as he rubbed his chin. "That sounds a little farfetched to me."

"It may be, but turn that off. We're getting out of here."

"Not yet! We still gotta..."

And then both Johnnie and I snapped our necks toward the hallway closet. A loud series of thuds came from behind the closed door. There was no way I'd believe a shoebox took a dive from top shelf to the floor.

Johnnie slowly turned his head toward me and said, "Did you say someone *was* here or someone *is* here?"

That, of course, had become the question of the hour.

Chapter 20

We tip-toed and crept as close to the closet door as possible. I initially drew my gun but then put it away thinking that gunshots coming from a dead man's apartment would've been too alarming.

I held my hand up toward Johnnie, who was at the door with a hand on the knob, ready to open it. I wanted him to wait a moment so I could dash into Hump's room and grab his steel bat. He slept with it every night, "Just in case..." as he put it.

The both of us stood in front of the closet, not knowing what to expect. Yeah, it could have been a rat in the closet or it could have been the person who found his way to Humpty's place before us. Whatever or whoever it was, I wanted to be prepared.

"On the count of three." I whispered to Johnnie. "You got it?"

Johnnie nodded his head. So I began the countdown.

"One... Two..."

I should have been quieter. Before I could get to "three" the door swung outward with such force that it hit Johnnie and he flew back into the wall, then the floor. The sound of his head crashing against it worried me.

Taking advantage of his surprise attack and the newly evened numbers, the intruder tackled me. Completely surprised, I felt like a scrawny wider receiver being flattened by a linebacker on steroids.

I tried to gather my senses and flip the guy on his back, but he wasn't having it. He grabbed me by my shirt and lifted me a few inches off of the floor. I was still a little groggy from the tackle. My eyes hadn't focused enough to make out his face.

But I did make out one thing. His fist. It was cocked back and ready to be unleashed.

A strong punch connected with my cheek. Pain shot through my jaw and traveled south to my neck and then north to my head.

Johnnie rolled onto his side, and that's when our guest decided to make a run for it. He sprinted to the front door of the apartment, snatched it open, and was gone. Johnnie and I were slumped on the floor like a pile of dirty laundry.

All we could do was look at each other. Startled. Trying to figure out if we were just hit by an express train.

Chapter 21

We got down to the street level and out of the building, hot on the heels of our mystery man. This guy was fast. I prayed that my jaw wasn't broken. The side of my face still throbbed from his earlier punch. I grimaced with every stride. But we had to catch him.

Strangers hiding in closets...it was clear now that Humpty's murder was a suspicious one. Questioning this man could lead us to some answers.

I watched him make a right turn into the alley at the end of Humpty's building. I made it there before Johnnie and waited the extra few seconds for him to catch up before going in. Johnnie reached me, nearly out of breath.

The mystery man hopped on top a green garbage dumpster and grabbed for the iron ladder connected to the fire escape. He was going back to the roof of the building.

"Go back in the building and meet me up top." I said to Johnnie.

"Back up?" He wrinkled his nose in protest.

"Go!" I yelled, running into the alley.

He reluctantly ran in the other direction, back toward the building's entrance.

By the time I got to the fire escape and started making my way up, our boy was two stories ahead of me. I was hoping that Johnnie was running as fast as he could. Maybe he'd get to the roof before either of us. Or at least meet me there in time to help with this guy.

I tried my best to close the gap, but it seemed like this guy wasn't tired or slowing down. There was a little favor on my part. His two-story lead had been cut to one by the time he reached the top.

When I got there, this guy was looking over the ledge of the roof, approximately a hundred feet away from me. Maybe he wanted to jump to the other building that was across the alley.

If this guy wasn't an Olympic long jumper, I'm pretty sure he would reconsider that thought. The alley was at least ten feet wide. But what really concerned me was the seven-story drop if he didn't make it. To jump, or not to jump? That was the question.

But low and behold, this fool was preparing to jump. He took a final look over the ledge and backed away about fifteen feet to get a running start. Rethinking his distance, he moved back another five feet. Doing my best Michael Johnson impersonation, I bolted in his direction. This allowed me to get closer to him. But not close enough. He still took off.

Running at full speed. He was nearly five feet away from the ledge and about to launch himself off of the rooftop. Seeing how close I was he decided to jump early. So did I. He jumped forward and I jumped from his left side.

As soon as his feet left the ground I drove my shoulder into his abdomen. This was my time to return the favor and tackle him. The force of my hit prevented him from going forward and we flew another few feet across the rooftop.

When we landed, the full force of my weight had rolled on top of him. He landed on his right shoulder and I heard a loud pop. He screamed in excruciating pain. I could only assume that the force of my tackle and his awkward landing popped his shoulder out of its socket.

With a dislocated shoulder, he was half the man he just was. Lying on top of him, I quickly grabbed that right shoulder and he cried out even louder in pain.

By this time, I was tired of the running, tired of the surprise attacks, and tired of feeling like I was in the dark concerning my good friend's murder. The mystery man was going to tell me something...or else.

I reached and grabbed my 9mm, which was still tucked snugly into a small holster I had around the back of my belt. The guy kept yelling.

I shoved the gun in his face and yelled, "Shut the fuck up!"

He didn't quite pipe down completely.

Sweat dripped down my face. My eyes started to burn a bit. I felt like it was time to start getting some answers.

"What were you doing in Humpty's apartment?!" I yelled.

No answer. There was only a fearful look in his eyes. His silent defiance threw me for a loop because I was waving a gun in his face. Was he scared of me, or something much worse? I couldn't tell.

Johnnie burst through the rooftop door, and the door swung all the way around and slammed into the wall.

Bam, loud as a gunshot, the noise caught me off guard. Sensing this, the guy used his good arm and punched me on the same chin he had blown up earlier. The throbbing returned, unbearable.

The force of the punch and the pain cause me to pulled back. The gun flew out of my hand. Johnnie was running toward me, but it was too late.

The mystery man successfully rolled from under me. And now that he was free, he got to his feet and was on the move again.

It didn't matter that he couldn't get a full running start. It didn't matter that we were only five feet away from the edge. None of that mattered. The mystery man ran and propelled himself forward.

He jumped.

Chapter 22

Johnnie and I watched as the unknown man soared through the air. If he wasn't an Olympic long jumper, he certainly was a jumper in high school or college.

It appeared that he was clearing the space between the buildings with ease. The two of us watched as our best chance at putting together these pieces escaped. I say escaped because I knew I wasn't going to make that jump and go after him. And even though Johnnie might do something dumb from time to time, I knew he wasn't going to make that leap either.

So the mystery man was undoubtedly getting away. Exhaustion and despair was starting to set in on me, until—

It had dawned on me that with a dislocated shoulder; there was no feasible way he would be able to extend both of his arms in front of him. He couldn't follow through with a jump like the one he was attempting.

And I was right, he couldn't. Midway in air, he thrust his chest toward the sky. His arms were extended behind him. But when it came time for him to throw both arms forward, he did it with his left, but his right arm dangled behind him and to his side.

He didn't have the momentum that would carry him through to the other rooftop. He cleared all but the last foot of distance. His body slammed against the red brick wall. His left arm flailed in an attempt at self-preservation. There was nothing between him and the asphalt of the alley, seven stories below.

Surprisingly, his one good arm landed on a metal lip, bolted into the side of the building. He flapped like a flag in the wind. It looked like he could make it, if he could pull himself up.

But once again, there was that dislocated shoulder. He tried to use his left arm hoist his body to safety, but it wasn't strong enough. He needed the aid of his other arm.

We watched as he tried to will movement in his dislocated arm, but it wasn't working. He was in pain and screamed. He swung the right side of his body upward, and screamed out in pain again.

There were two bolts attaching the metal lip to the red brick. The rocking of his body, back and forth, caused one bolt to loosen and then rip from the brick.

The metal lip now paralleled the building. The mystery man was hanging on for dear life. Johnnie and I looked on in a horror, knowing what was coming next.

We watched his hand slide along the metal until he had no more to cling to. His body cut the air on its way toward the ground. This time he didn't yell or scream. His body made contact, with the sound of crunching and splintering bones echoing up seven stories to the rooftop.

Maybe jumping wasn't the brightest idea.

Chapter 23

I couldn't understand why Johnnie was lagging behind. We had to go! After making our way down from the roof, I wasted no time, walking in the opposite direction of the pile of blood and death spread about in the alley.

Johnnie walked at half of my pace. He was constantly looking over his shoulder too. "Where are we going?" he asked.

I didn't answer or look back at him. My lack of response must have put a sense of urgency in his step. I heard him double time it to catch up to me.

We were at least three and a half blocks away from the alley. Johnnie spun me around by my shoulder. Grabbing me like that, he was lucky that I didn't punch him in his face. I was trying to put the pieces of the puzzle together and nothing was making sense.

My head hurt like hell. I didn't know if it was the stress of our circumstances or from being hit earlier. But either way, I wasn't in the mood. To say I was irritated would have been an understatement.

"Where are we going, Anthony? He's back that way!"

"He's dead. There's nothing he can tell us."

"I know he's dead, but there's gotta be something we can..."

I wouldn't let him finish his sentence. "I guess you're right, I suppose. Maybe we can search the dead man's pockets or his wallet to get some info that'll tell us something.

"And you know what...maybe we'll also get some magical force field that'll come down from the sky, and cover us so that we can't be seen, while we search a dead man in the wide open public!"

Johnnie looked like he was about to raise his voice in protest, once again.

"He's dead!" I said firmly. "And in a situation like this, that means dead-end. There's nothing he can tell us. There's probably a huge crowd around him by now, I'm sure the cops have already been called, and God forbid there are security cameras in the area.

"So would you like to go back and risk getting identified or caught, and for nothing? Or would you rather regroup and think of another way to get the answers we need? The man is dead and we're almost out of options."

"This is the closest we've been and I can taste it. I don't give a damn what you say, I'm going back." Johnnie turned and started walking back toward the alley.

By this time I was fed up. I was tired of Johnnie and his selfish ways. How could he not see that returning to the alley wouldn't do anything but get him arrested?

"Going back?" I asked. "Really?! Well then be honest. For what? Why do you *really* want to go back?"

Johnnie stopped, but didn't respond.

"You gonna make me say it, huh? Ok, fuck it...this has more to do with your father than it does Humpty!

"Here we have a job to do, and you're willing to go at it alone, with silly ass ideas, thinking that if you can strike gold, you can be the hero. And then your father might change his mind about the houses. But we have a fuckin' job to do Johnnie!

"This isn't about the houses! But since you think it is, then guess what? You're the same fuckin' Johnnie, doing things the same fuckin' way. And you know what that means? No gambling houses for you. Ever."

Johnnie took a minute to think about what I said. He took another look back at the commotion that was bubbling three and a half blocks away, and he knew I was right.

"It does look kinda busy down there," Johnnie finally said in a conversational tone. "Ok. Let's go."

He pulled me by my collar and led me away from the madness that was quickly surrounding the dead man in the alley. As we got further down the street, he said. "We're not completely out of options...we have at least fifteen minutes to make our way to Skinny Vinnie's."

And he was absolutely right. I completely forgot about Skinny Vinnie from Southeast. But we were in Northwest DC, the other side of town, and I wasn't quite sure if fifteen minutes was enough time for us to get to him.

Chapter 24

Southeast DC. This was the only quadrant within the District of Columbia where gentrification hadn't caught up. It was still a high drug and crime area that was heavily populated by blacks. When gentrification does finally make its way across the Anacostia River, these black people would then be forced to move on the other side of the border, into Maryland's Prince Georges County.

But for now, it was still full of corner boys, carryouts and liquor stores. And Vinnie's home was right in the middle of it. He lived in a small two-bedroom home his grandmother had left to him upon her death. His family was one of the few white ones that lived in Southeast. You could probably count them on one hand.

Vinnie's home was on Howard Road, a few houses in from Martin Luther King Jr. Avenue. And this avenue was like so many other MLK avenues, roads, and drives in every city across America. Broken down and in disrepair.

The night had been tiring and full of surprises. All I wanted to do was grab Vinnie and get back to the restaurant. I looked down at my watch and we were ten minutes past the deadline Vinnie gave us. I hoped he had changed his mind, or at least wasn't a punctual person.

After walking up to the front door, I rang the bell and waited for a response.

"Ring it again," Johnnie said. He was standing behind me. "He might not have heard it."

That was wishful thinking, I was almost certain that Vinnie was long gone. He was probably sitting on a bus headed out of the city, while we were standing at his home ringing a doorbell in vain. But to oblige Johnnie, I rang the bell two more times. There was still no response.

"Ok. That's that. Let's go." I turned away from the house to leave.

"What do you mean? We haven't even gone in."

"The last time we tried something like that, we didn't have the best of luck. Vinnie's probably halfway to Kalamazoo by now. Let's go back to the restaurant and tell your father what we know before this thing gets out of control. Let them figure out the rest."

Johnnie pouted with disagreement. "Anthony, it's already out of control."

I knew he was right. I turned to look at the door. And shook my head.

"Damn it, Johnnie. So now *you're* gonna start talking sense into *me*, I see. Keep a look out."

I knelt at the doorknob and took a narrow rectangular black pouch out of my back pocket. I made it a habit of keeping an eight-piece lock pick set on me at all times. I positioned the torque wrench at the bottom of the keyhole and slipped the pick in along the top.

Feeling around for each pin within the lock, I positioned my knee against the door for a little extra support. Without warning, it became clear that I didn't need my lock picking tools. The weight I placed on the door forced it to open. And it did so with ease.

I threw my hands out in front of me to stop myself from falling flat on my face. I quickly got to my feet and looked at Johnnie in disbelief.

"What the hell?" I exclaimed.

"Nobody leaves their front door unlocked in Southeast DC."

Which was completely true. Either Skinny was in such a big hurry he didn't bother to lock it, or someone else had been here. Or was here. Whatever the reason, my gun came out once again.

"Alright, Johnnie. You wanted in. Now we're in."

Chapter 25

Johnnie had drawn his gun as well, thanks to lessons we learned from our last encounter with the stranger at Humpty's place. We decided we'd rather be safe than sorry.

Based on previous experience, we started with the hallway closet before moving throughout the house.

"You open the door," I whispered.

Johnnie nodded in agreement. Once I was set, he snatched the door open. Nobody was in the closet.

"Ok. I'll check the kitchen," Johnnie said.

"Why? You hungry?"

"Real funny." He peeked past the kitchen portal after hitting the light switch.

After the kitchen, we checked the living room, den, both bedrooms and all other closets. No windows were open. No intruder was in the home. And more importantly, Skinny Vinnie was nowhere to be found.

Johnnie resigned himself to the idea that we would leave empty handed, and so did I. We put away our weapons and now we were more ready than ever to leave.

But before we could walk out, Johnnie said, "Hold up, where's the john?"

"You're right," I responded. "We didn't even check the bathroom."

"Check the bathroom? Man, I've gotta pee!"

We both walked through the home, looking for the bathroom. It was hidden in plain sight, in between the bedrooms. I reached for the door, but before I could open it, Johnnie motioned for me to grab my gun, just in case.

I pointed the gun in front of me, pushed open the door, and Johnnie quickly hit the light switch. Once the light was on, we realized why we couldn't find Skinny Vinnie. He was lying, facedown, in a pool of his own blood.

"Damn." I wrinkled my nose. "Another dead body."

Johnnie was no stranger to dead bodies, but I think the manner in which this one was handled bothered him. Vinnie's stomach was sliced open the same as Humpty's. What made this scene different was Vinnie's face.

His face had been bashed to the point where it was unrecognizable. The crow bar, that I assumed was used to do the damage, was lying on the floor next to his body.

The only way Vinnie could be identified was by a tattoo he had centered on his back, just below his neck. We had all seen it in the past. It was a compass.

The letters E, S, W were clearly marked, indicating the directions of east, south, and west. But instead of the letter N to indicate the northern direction, there was a large fleur-de-lis pointing north, in its place.

I put my gun away with a sigh. That was that. In one night, we came across an intruder at Humpty's, who fell to his death. And then we come here to find the person who was to help us put these pieces together, murdered. Did the guy who attacked us murder him? Is this coincidence? Or just bad luck and timing?

Whatever the answers were, we wouldn't get them here and we wouldn't get them tonight. I grabbed a hand towel that was hanging near the sink and tossed it to Johnnie.

"Wipe down everything we put our hands on."

While he was off removing our fingerprints, I took out my camera phone and took some pictures of Skinny Vinnie's body. I'd delete the photos later, after Marco had a chance to see them.

Three dead bodies, in total. By the way Humpty and Vinnie were cut up, I'd say they were definitely killed by the same guy. And assuming the dead guy in the alley was a different guy, then the machete-man was still out there.

I had a feeling that one day soon, we would meet him. I was only hoping that the meeting would be on our terms and not his.

Chapter 26

Back at restaurant, Johnnie and I filled in Marco and Nick Nick with all the gory details of our night. Marco took some time to absorb all of the information.

"This is indeed unfortunate." Marco huffed and shook his head. "Do you think we can we avoid violence? What are our chances?" He directed the question to Nick Nick.

"I say our chances of avoiding violence are higher than they appear," Nick Nick said.

Johnnie flashed a look of astonishment while his father showed no reaction to Nick Nick's assessment. Johnnie was about to step forward to say something, but I grabbed him by his arm and shook my head.

This was a moment where we needed to be seen and not heard. If for whatever reason, they felt like they needed our opinion, they would certainly ask us for it.

"I don't know, three bodies in one week. Looks like they're just getting started."

Johnnie was relieved to see that his father was thinking along the same lines that he was.

"Look at it like this," Nick Nick continued in my direction. "These guys know that we're on to them.

There's no way they'll fess up to killing Humpty and trying to kill you. But since your little visit with Marty, they must be worried that you'll figure it out."

"So they're cleaning house then," Marco chimed in. "Get whatever info they can from Humpty's place and eliminate anyone who could tie them to anything."

Nick Nick turned his attention back Marco. "Exactly. They're not coming after us. They're trying to make sure we don't have a concrete reason to come after them. They're scared."

It made sense to me. And I was glad that Johnnie was getting a chance to see how his father and Nick Nick reasoned their way through situations before jumping to conclusions. I was hoping the experience would rub off on him and he'd be able to do the same.

"This is good to know. Hopefully, they'll begin to unravel soon enough. Then I will be there to pull that last piece of string that's hanging out. We're going to stick with the plan, gentlemen. No more gambling houses for us. But I will address their horrible lapse in judgment, when the time is right.

"For now, Nick Nick, I want you to call your guy at the police department. Give them Skinny Vinnie's address. Maybe that will put some heat on Oronzio and his people."

Nick Nick nodded. "Anything else?" he asked.

"No. That's it. And boys..." He said toward the two of us. "I want you two on your way to getting some rest. You've had a long day and this is far from over."

"Sure, Marco," I said.

"Anything you say, Pop," Johnnie said immediately after.

"That'll be all, gentlemen." Which was everyone's cue to leave.

Johnnie and I reached the door and Nick Nick wasn't far behind. I held the door open for him. It would have been rude to let it close in his face.

"Nick Nick. Hold on," Marco said. "On second thought, there is something else I want you to do." Marco looked at the door. It was a sign for us to leave.

Johnnie and I backed out the office to let the grown folks talk. Marco and Nick Nick were huddled. I guess whatever it was they needed to discuss, wasn't for our ears.

Chapter 27

Three nights later, Oronzio and Marty Fucker stood outside of Tommy's Tavern, on the corner of Massachusetts Avenue and Third Street, in the prestigious Capitol Hill neighborhood.

Marty checked his watch and looked at Oronzio.

"Give him another five minutes," Oronzio said. "Then we'll go in."

They were there to meet with the other bosses and it appeared that they were going to be late. Crime bosses meeting in the shadow of the US Capitol, the irony wasn't lost on Oronzio.

Hypocritical bastards, he thought to himself. In his opinion, the United States government was the biggest crime organization in the world.

Less than sixty seconds later, Oronzio could see Nick Nick walking down the street from the direction of Union Station, while Marty was looking the other way.

"He's here," he said. "Keep your eyes open."

"Are you kidding me?" Marty said. "He's by himself and he's old, at that."

"He's Dominic Nicholas. Don't fool yourself. He'll eat you for dinner and your hatchets for dessert."

Caution was the name of the game for Oronzio.

"I see you made it," Oronzio called out to Nick Nick, as he approached. "We have a bit of business to tend to tonight, and I was getting worried you'd miss us."

Nick Nick and Oronzio shook hands. Nick Nick nodded toward Marty. "I'm sure you weren't worried. No need for condescension."

Marty narrowed his gaze. "No need for confrontation either." He shot back. The tension between them was heavy.

Oronzio turned around to look at Marty with scolding eyes. "Enough Fucker. Why don't you go inside and tell 'em to give me a couple minutes."

Marty was intent on having a staring match with Nick Nick. "Hmm," he said. "Yeah. I can do that."

He looked the unflinching Nick Nick up and down, and left the two alone.

"Ok. Let's get down to it," Oronzio said. "You called me."

"I'll make this quick. You're supposed to go in there and talk to everyone about Marco's plan to leave the business."

"That I am."

"But here's the problem. Marco doesn't feel you're going to give your best effort on his behalf."

Nick Nick was correct but Oronzio didn't say or do anything that would confirm his statement. He waited for Nick Nick to continue.

"You can be a persuasive man, when you want to be. And simply put, he wants you to convince them. Because when it's all said and done, Marco isn't asking anyone for their permission. He's leaving."

Oronzio took a minute to consider what had just been said to him.

"If I do this," Oronzio said. "What's in it for me?"

"For you, Marco is prepared to brush aside any disagreement between you two. There'll be clean slate."

"That's it? That's pretty bland!"

"Will two million dollars add a little flavor?" Nick Nick asked. "A clean slate and a fat pocket. That's what he's offering."

"And all I have to do is use my aforementioned skills of persuasion?"

"That's it. Yes? Or no? I need to know right now."

Oronzio stood there and did his best impersonation of the Thinker statue, but he had already come to a decision. His mind was made up some time ago.

"Ok," he said. "Tell Marco he has a deal."

Nick Nick cracked his first smile. "That's good to know. I'll leave you to your business so I can go tell him. One last thing, to show that there are no hard feelings, Marco wants to host everybody next week for a final night of fun. He'll comp all the bosses fifty grand in chips. Everyone else will have to see the bank."

"Sounds good. I can't wait. With Marco retired," Oronzio said, "what are you going to do? My door is opened to you. I've always appreciated your professionalism."

"I'll be just fine. My plans are my plans."

The two shook hands again and parted ways. But before Oronzio entered the building, he called back to Nick Nick.

"You sure you don't want to come in? For old time's sake."

Nick Nick didn't respond, as he walked off. And Oronzio knew he wouldn't. This was a life that Marco's organization was intent on leaving behind.

And Oronzio thought that Marco must have been a fool to believe he would get any help from him. Even though, for a clean slate and two million, Oronzio said he would.

But Oronzio would do no such thing. His mind had already been made up.

Chapter 28

By the time Oronzio reached the private parlor in the back, smoke must have been rising from his head. That's how angry he was. Marco thinks he can buy me? *The nerve of this man*, he thought.

Aside from the parlor, the tavern was completely empty. Tommy made sure of it. Everyone sat around a banquet table.

Oronzio composed himself and opened the door. The meeting hadn't started yet because they were waiting on him. Seated at the table were three others. If Marco were present, the five of them would have represented DC's most notorious illegitimate entrepreneurs. Its' diversity reflected the newfound diversity of Washington, DC.

In this new District of Columbia, everyone had a shot at making it big on the underground scene. This was true as long as you had the resources to grow your criminal enterprise and the power to protect it.

Those sitting around the table each had a particular niche. This is what kept the peace between everybody. There was no need to infringe upon someone else's business because they each were making a fortune in their own lanes.

Carlos Fernandez, Jr. or Carilto to family and close friends. He was born to upper middle class Puerto Rican parents in Montgomery County, Maryland, but had crafted a convincing story about being an immigrant from Columbia.

Using his "Columbian" connections, he was able to acquire and distribute the majority of the cocaine that was sold within the city limits.

Across from Carlito sat Tommy Callahan, owner of Tommy's Tavern. But not just the one they were in. He single handedly grew and franchised the establishment. There were nine other taverns in the District, Maryland and Virginia.

Everyone at the table used Tommy to launder their money. For a percentage, he would take the money earned through illegal means, filter it through the business operations of his taverns and provide clean, spendable and investible money in return.

Last but not least was the heavy hitter. The person that no one at the table would dare cross. Her name was Marina Milkovich. Marina controlled high-end prostitution in town. The DC Madame, who was arrested years earlier, had nothing on Marina. Or as her girls would call her, *Mother Mary* or *Mother May I.*

It was even rumored that Marina was the one who orchestrated the DC Madame's arrest in order to eliminate her competition. And that was a rumor everybody believed.

Unlike everyone else in the room, Marina didn't have the natural inclination for illegal activity. Marina had stumbled into it.

She and her husband Dmitry had migrated to America when they were both twenty-three years old. They hadn't been married two years. After unsuccessfully attempting to find employment, Dmitry and Marina had been kicked out of the apartment they were renting. They were starving and living in a downtrodden homeless shelter.

That's when Dmitry had enough. He reconnected with a childhood friend who had risen quickly in the underground Russian mob in the states. In no time, the work he got enabled him to make enough money to provide a comfortable life for he and his wife.

For years, Dmitry worked in different capacities for his bosses. He managed drug distribution, loan sharking, protection, and prostitution. Once given the permission to step out and work on his own, he decided to focus on one area and become an expert. Prostitution was his crime of choice.

Marina stood in the shadows and watched for decades as her husband ran his business. And as long as he was able to provide, she really didn't care about his occupational responsibilities.

She was desensitized to it. It was Dmitry's practice to sleep with every new girl, in order to assess her sexual strengths and weaknesses. Marina convinced herself that it was just part of the job.

Unexpectedly at the age of forty-nine, Dmitry suffered a heart attack and died, while he was auditioning a new girl. Once again, after his death and with no source of income, Marina found herself broke and on the verge of losing her home.

What pushed her over the edge was when the Attorney General, operating a campaign to crack down on the sex crimes, threatened to put her in jail if she didn't give up the names of all the girls who had been working for her husband. Many of those girls, Marina had come to adore, as if they were her own children.

Sitting in her husbands' immaculate home office she rummaged through his desk and found nothing. He would be ashamed of her for the mess she made of his space, she thought. Calling Dmitry a neat freak would have been an understatement. She looked high and low. There was no list of names.

Trying to get mentally prepared for her impending arrest, she convinced herself that jail would be better than living in a ratty homeless shelter again. At least she would have a roof over her head and three meals a day.

Marina let her head hang before resting it on the desk. Her chin sat on her folded arms. Staring across the room, she saw something that struck her as odd and out of place. It was the painted portrait of Marina.

She was twenty-five years old in the portrait and her beauty wasn't far off, even being close to fifty. But the painting was crooked.

The position of the painting was tilted. As she approached it, she noticed the discoloration of the wall. It could have been from the portrait hanging there for some time, she thought. But the closer she got, the more she realized that that wasn't the case.

She moved the painting aside to find a hidden door. And behind the hidden door was a safe. Looking at the safe, she immediately knew that the combination would be the month, day and year of her birth. It was the only combination Dmitry had ever used. And *viola*, it opened.

Inside the safe was a handgun, what she counted out to be one hundred thousand dollars in cash, and three ledgers, all containing names of the girls who worked for her husband. What made it better: the names were listed alphabetically, by the men who paid for their services.

Halfway down the second page of the first ledger she saw a familiar name. *Aigeldinger, Jonathan R.* He was the Attorney General who threatened to throw her in jail. There was no mistaking his name.

The next day Marina marched in the Attorney Generals office unannounced. Two beauties, Veronica and Cheryl, flanked her.

"Could you excuse us?" She asked the two men sitting in Aigeldinger's office.

"Mrs. Milkovich!" Aigeldinger protested. "You do not have an appointment. You'll have to leave this..."

He cut his own statement off as soon as he recognized the girls who were with Marina. His tone changed and he quickly asked the men to his office.

"What's the meaning of this, Mrs. Milkovich?"

Without waiting for an invitation, Marina took a seat. Veronica and Cheryl remained standing. She leaned across Aigeldinger's desk and said, "I found them. The whole list. All of them. And I also have a list of all the clients."

Aigeldinger cleared his throat, as if he was about to talk.

"Shut up!" Marina said. "You're going to leave me the hell alone. Because if you don't, the media will find out that the Attorney General likes to have Cheryl suck his dick while Veronica shoves anal beads in his ass. You got it?"

Aigeldinger didn't say a word.

"And let me make this clear. I have duplicates in safekeeping and they're all ready to go if anything happens to me. So choose your future actions wisely.

You're not the only big fish on that client list. There are much bigger fish, with much higher pay grades and more influence than you. And they all like a little attention, from time to time.

"So if you don't want to be known as the asshole who brought down everyone from the mayor's office to the White House, then you leave me the hell alone."

From that point on, Marina never had a problem. Not from anyone. Not the cops, lawyers, judges or politicians. And why would she? She reopened her husband's business and ran it as affectively as he had. Marina even kept up Dmitry's auditioning tactic of sleeping with new girls to assess their sexual strengths and weaknesses.

Once Marina walked out of that office, she made a vow to herself. She would never allow her security to be compromised by another person again. Running her husband's business afforded her the autonomy to chart her own course. And she would never let anyone take that away.

Never.

Chapter 29

"Is everything going to be ok?" Marina asked Oronzio.

"No."

"Care to explain?"

Tommy had brought in a round of drinks for everyone and Carilto was sitting up in his seat.

"Marco's mind is made up. He's keeping his promise to close the gambling houses. In actuality, they're already closed. But he is opening a house for one last party night next week. He's invited everyone. Even comping us fifty thousand a piece."

"Well." Marina tapped her fingernails on the table. "That's unfortunate. Ok. You know what needs to be done, right?"

Knowing exactly what Marina was insinuating, Carlito spoke up for the first time. "Hold up. Isn't that taking it too far? This is Marco we're talking about. The man has been there for each of us at some point and time. I don't think there's any need for something permanent. Just let the man be on his way."

Marina shook her head. "No. This is the way it has to be. You ever hear of the Racketeer Influenced and Corrupt Organizations Act?"

"What?" Carlito asked.

"Of course you haven't, my fake Columbian friend."

"RICO," Tommy interjected. "It's called the RICO Act."

"Precisely." Marina accented her word by pointing. "Who's to say that Marco isn't visited by the ghost of Christmas past one night? And then all of a sudden he grows a conscious and wants to come clean about prior crimes. Once the Feds step in, we're all done. We clean our money through that one man." Marina jabbed her finger in Tommy's direction. "And because of that we all can be charged as one criminal organization, because of RICO."

Marina sat back in her chair. "Now who wants to risk that? Not I. Whether you like him or not, there's a risk that jail time is in our future, so long as he isn't here at the table with us. And because of that, Marco has got to die."

Marina stopped long enough to register agreement on everyone's face. She made a quick and clear case.

"Ok. Then it's settled. Let's make sure this last little gambling hoorah next week is Marco's going away party."

Oronzio's eyes narrowed with anticipation as a grin squiggled along the bottom part of his face. Hearing this was music to his ears.

Chapter 30

Since finding Skinny Vinnie with his face bashed in, I had been working at the restaurant every night. We were also neck deep into planning the logistics for the final shebang at the gambling house and I was in need of a break. I needed just one night of relaxing without gunshots, breaking into homes, and dead bodies.

I had arranged for some quality time with Coco at her favorite DC eatery, Ben's Chili Bowl on the U Street Corridor. Even though I didn't feel like being anywhere near the restaurant, that's where we were. I kept looking over my shoulder, hoping Johnnie wouldn't frantically interrupt us with some last minute emergency, needing my attention. I had crossed my fingers and knocked on the wooden table, hoping he wouldn't.

The place smelled of half smokes, hamburgers and French fries, and it was packed. Being a national historical landmark, everyone wanted some of the famous Ben's Chili Bowl. And not to mention, the food was mouth-watering. I was shocked that we were even able to get a booth.

"You really going in on those half smokes."

"Mind your business," Coco snapped at me.

"I'm just saying." I chuckled. "Do you inhale your food like that on all your dates?"

"So this is a date, Mr. Jones? You must think I'm pretty cheap. A half smoke and some chili-cheese fries, huh?"

"Actually two half smokes," I said with a grin. "...and some chili-cheese fries."

Coco balled up a napkin and threw it at me. But for real, she truly packed it in, which was nothing new. I never understood where all the food went. Her figure remained flawless. At least it was how I liked it. The nicest coke bottle I had ever seen.

After finishing the last piece of her half smoke, she grabbed her lemonade and iced tea mixed drink and got up from her seat. Within a second flat, she sat on my side of the booth, shoving me closer to the wall. She wrapped her arm in mine and pulled me closer.

"I'm glad we're spending a little time together, sir."

"Well, we could spend more time together, if you liked to."

"So it's up to me?" she asked. "I highly doubt it's that simple."

I looked at her and shrugged my shoulders as to say, "Maybe it is, maybe it isn't."

She leaned in and kissed me on my lips. It felt an hour long. The room became quiet and everyone disappeared for that moment in time.

After her warm and inviting kiss, she said, "I'd like that."

But I could tell a "*but*" was coming.

"But," she began. "There are still unanswered questions."

I knew this was coming sooner or later. I had given some thought as to how I'd address it but hadn't settled on an approach. And now it felt like whatever future I could have with Coco hinged on my coming clean.

But I knew better. Coming clean would only invite more questions. And instead of bringing her closer, it would only end up pushing her away.

"Who is Anthony Ribisi?" Coco asked. "If you don't want to tell me, at least tell me to mind my business. Then I'll know you don't want to go any further with me."

"'Mind your business.' For Christ sakes, that sounds a bit harsh."

"No harsher than being ignored. Or lied to."

Coco was right. I owed her the truth. And if the truth was that I didn't want to talk about it, then "Mind your business" would probably be the most appropriate response. But I wasn't quite sure it was the response I wanted to gamble with.

The silence between us was telling. My phone rang, breaking the stillness. I didn't recognize the number so I sent the call to voicemail.

Still. There were no words.

"Ok. Well at least tell me this; does it have anything to do with that restaurant you work at? He *is* Marco *Ribisi*, isn't he?"

My phone rang again. It was the same unrecognized phone number. I picked the phone up, sent the call to voicemail again, and this time switched it to vibrate.

I think I was more comfortable being subtly rude by not answering her questions, rather than overtly rude by answering a phone while we were on our "date."

"Alright. I'll try this another way, and please don't be mad at me."

Anytime someone warned me not to be mad at them before saying or doing whatever it was they were about to say or do, I automatically prepared myself to be mad.

"Does it have anything to do with the gun I found in your closet?"

"You went through my closet!" I shot back. "You shouldn't have done that, Coco! You ever hear about privacy and respecting people's boundaries?!"

Another call came in from the same number. It vibrated so hard that it shook the table. Once again, I pressed the button along the top of the phone, sending it to voicemail.

"I'm sorry, Jelani! No! No, I don't know anything about privacy. I'm just plain nosey! But that's not the point." She stopped in order to get her tone under control and then she whispered sternly, "You had a gun! And I'm scared for you."

"Well, don't be."

"I've asked around about that Marco Ribisi, and I tell you, I don't like what I heard. Illegal gambling and drugs! I don't like it."

I couldn't help but roll my eyes. "Well..." I said. "You should only believe half of what you hear from the streets."

"Oh really?! And which half is it?"

I let a moment of stillness pass between us. An uncomfortable silence. Measuring my words carefully, I said, "The only thing you need to know about Marco Ribisi is that without him, I wouldn't be here. Without him, I would have been strung out, in jail, or dead in a ditch somewhere. That's all you need to know. Other than that, the man should be a ghost to you.

"Now I'd really appreciate it, if you never brought his name up again."

Measured. I wanted my words to make clear what Marco meant to me, and that this was a discussion I didn't care to have again. It hurt me to take such a tone with her, but I thought it was best to end any idea of further discussion about Marco.

Coco pulled away from me, her face painted with disappointment. Water began to well at the bottom of her eyes. Then my phone vibrated again. It buzzed at least five times, but I was caught up in watching Coco process my words and the tone in which I spoke them to her.

Then my phone vibrated again. I was so upset that I barely heard or felt it. It buzzed at least five times.

Coco said, "Maybe you better answer it." As she got up and moved back to where she first sat.

"Hello." My voice came across flat and cold.

"H..Hello?" Someone stuttered on the other end. "Is this Anthony?"

After the discussion I just had with Coco, I didn't want to say that name, so all I said was, "Speaking."

"Man...I really need you to come get me. Can you come get me? Like right now."

Clearly, not in the mood for mystery calls, my response was, "Come get you? Who the hell is this?"

"It's me, Anthony. It's Skinny Vinnie."

And just like that, he was back from the dead. But how? Both Johnnie and I saw his dead body. Unless that wasn't his body at all.

"Where are you?" I asked him. "Ok. Don't move. I'm on my way."

I hung up the phone and saw the disappointment on Coco's face turn into frustration.

"I guess you're leaving."

I didn't say anything in return. Then she followed up with, "Fine, *Anthony*..." intentionally using that name. "Do what you have to do."

I tried to be as apologetic as possible. Apologetic for the tone I took with her. Apologetic for nearly making her cry. Apologetic for what I was about to do next.

"I'm so sorry. I've gotta go." She took her turn at being nonresponsive. She picked up her purse and pulled herself out of the booth. I stood up with her.

Then she finally spoke. But only to stick a dagger in my heart. "I guess it's good we came in our own cars, huh?"

She didn't wait for a reply. She didn't offer a hug or a kiss. She carried herself out of Ben's Chili Bowl, without even looking back.

Chapter 31

Barreling through the doors of the main hall at Union Station, we quickly made our way to the Amtrak waiting area. After scanning the crowd, Johnnie saw Skinny Vinnie, exactly where he said he'd be. He was sitting in a seat to the far left of us, closest to the men's restroom.

The two of us were floored by this turn of events. Since Johnnie had been ready to bet his life that this guy could connect all the dots for us, finding him alive was both shocking and exhilarating.

Now, our only job was to get Vinnie safely back to the restaurant and connect the dots that would set everything on clearer path. I wasn't completely sold on the idea that Vinnie had the answer to whether Humpty was killed by Oronzio or not.

Would he ever lead us to finding out why Humpty was murdered? I didn't know, but we needed answers.

"Hey!" Skinny Vinnie yelled, waving us over. "Thank God!"

"Skinny. We thought you was..." Johnnie began. But I place a hand on him and shook my head. It was obvious to us that someone had been murdered at Vinnie's house.

But if he was unaware, I didn't want to lead with that type of revelation.

"Get me out of here, fellas."

"Hold on first. You said you were being followed. Are you sure?" I asked, looking around the waiting area.

"Yes!" Vinnie whisper-yelled, under his breath, attempting not to draw any more attention to him.

"Ok. Where are they then?" Johnnie asked.

Skinny Vinnie whipped his head from side to side, surveying the room. "It was two of them," he said with another snap of the head. "Two white boys." He snapped his head to the other side. "One was bald with a mustache and beard, but the other had a full head of hair. Regular cut.

"Baldie was wearing dark blues jeans and uh... a black t-shirt and short leather jacket." He said that with a snap of his fingers. "The other was in a navy blue suit. With pinstripes. They were just here!"

"And you're sure they were following you?" I asked. "Why?"

"Because I know who killed Humpty." He pointed to himself.

Johnnie and I started inspecting the crowd in an attempt to locate the men who were following Skinny Vinnie. I didn't see anyone matching the descriptions he gave.

I left Johnnie with the trembling stick figure of a man and walked out of the waiting area. I thought it was possible I'd have a better chance of spotting them if I moved around. It wasn't a busy night at the station. Being nearly eleven o'clock, there were only a few people looking to catch late night trains and buses. Aside from the McDonald's, the rest of the retail shops had closed or were about to shut down.

I saw approximately twenty-five people, either seated or coming and going. The only other noticeable people were four Amtrak police officers standing by the police kiosk, across from the Starbucks. One had a bomb sniffing German shepherd on a leash and the other three wore M-16 rifles strapped over their shoulders.

I didn't want to look suspicious around the police, so I calmly walked passed them, around to the ticket counters, and through the hall on the other side. This brought me closer to the McDonald's and the women's restroom. Making my way back to the guys made a full circuit, and during that time, I hadn't seen the mystery men.

When I got back, Johnnie was doing his best to keep Skinny Vinnie calm. "I don't see anyone," I said. "Let's go."

"Where we going?" Vinnie asked. I didn't answer him. I took him by his arm and led him to the entrance of the waiting area. We were about to walk past the police, toward the main hall, and then out of Union Station, but I noticed something when I looked to my right.

Baldie and the man in the suit had stepped out from around the corner, near the Sbarro pizza restaurant to our right. When I did my trek through the station, I had gone in the opposite direction, which is probably why I hadn't seen them earlier.

I stopped, grabbed Johnnie, and the three of us looked in their direction. My eyes locked with the guy in the navy blue suit and they too stopped walking. But only for a brief moment. If they had anything to do with Humpty's murder, I could only assume they recognized me and Johnnie. The man in the navy blue suit looked toward his partner and nodded his head. And there was a grin on the bald one's face. They knew who we were.

"That's them!" Vinnie whispered into my shoulder. He tried to hide while shivering at the same time.

"No shit!" Johnnie whispered back. "We can't go anywhere if they're gonna follow us."

They were getting closer and closer to us and I didn't want to play this game any longer. We needed to get a move on, but we needed them off of our back for that to happen. Navy blue suit guy pulled his blazer back slightly and ran his fingers along the protruding handle of his gun. He did this until he noticed the Amtrak police. Then they just walked our way.

Ten feet away and coming closer. Five feet away and almost in front of our faces. Now they were standing directly in front of us while we stood at the entrance of the waiting area.

Baldie said, "Excuse us." They brushed pass us and walked into the waiting area, nearly knocking me over in the process. *These guys were really starting to piss me off.*

Johnnie and Vinnie looked at each other and then looked back at the two men, who were now seated about twenty feet away and staring. "How are we getting out of here?" Johnnie asked.

"Right out that front door," I said to the guys. "This is what I want you to do. Wait sixty seconds and then walk to the main hall. Go straight out the door and to the car. I'll meet you there. But remember, sixty seconds."

"Sixty seconds. Got it," Johnnie said.

Before he finished talking, I was already on my way to the bathroom, which was only about fifteen feet away. I was hoping that the men following Skinny Vinnie would remain focused on their prize.

Once inside the bathroom, I lined my body against the wall, praying I couldn't be seen. I still had a decent view of the waiting area. It took about thirty more seconds, but on cue, Johnnie and Vinnie were on their way. And just as I thought, after taking a look toward the restroom, presumably for me, the men got up and started following their prize. They were being led by a carrot on a stick.

I came out the restroom and walked past the now empty police kiosk, then walked toward two of the four police officers patrolling the area near the baggage carousel.

"Excuse me, sir!" I said, waving at them. They looked at each other and then made their way to me. "Listen, I don't mean to be overly cautious," I said. "But I keep seeing these posters around, 'See something. Say something,' ya know. Because of terrorism and all."

"That's right," One of the officers said sternly.

"Well, I don't know what's up with those two guys right there." I pointed down the hall, at the two following Johnnie and Vinnie. "I was in the bathroom with them and they were acting a little suspicious. Like scary suspicious. I just handled my biz and got out of there. But when I saw them outside the bathroom, I know I saw a gun in the waistband of the guy in the suit."

"A gun, you say?" the other officer said. "Are you sure?"

"I did Marine ROTC in college, man." A believable lie that I was hoping would give me some creditability. Then I said, "Because of training, I've been around a bunch of guns. I know a gun when I see it."

And that was all it took. I followed them as they jogged to catch up with two armed men. The officers were right behind them just before they reached the main hall. I kept my distance but could hear them talking on the radio to the other two officers. "Set a post at the entrance!" I heard one of them yell into his walkie-talkie.

Everyone was now in the main hall. Two officers and a dog were at the front door. Johnnie and Vinnie were about to walk past them. Baldie and navy blue suit guy behind them. And I was trailing the two officers I had spoken with.

Johnnie and Vinnie were now out of the building and the guys following were about to walk through the doors as well. But one of the two officers standing at the front held out a hand and said, "Hold on right there sir. We have a few questions for you."

By this time, the other officers and I had closed in. The Amtrak police surrounded Baldie and navy blue suit guy. I stared at them as I walked past and out the door. A look of frustrated surprise was all over their faces.

The last thing I heard was the bark of a dog and one of the police yelling, "Gun! Get down on the ground!" The other officers were yelling, "Get down!" as well. Those commands trailed outside of the door as it closed.

I smiled as I pictured the men dropping to the floor, lying face down.

Johnnie was standing at the car and Skinny Vinnie was already seated in the back. Johnnie's mouth was wide open. "How in the hell? We walked right out the front door!"

I looked back at him and said, "See something. Say something." I hopped behind the wheel of the car, and we were off.

Chapter 32

Fifteen minutes later we were at the restaurant. I called Marco before going to Union Station so he was there waiting for us. The place was empty.

Once in Marco's office, Vinnie couldn't sit still. He sat down, stood up, and then frantically paced the floor. All the moving around led me to think he might have been high. If I hadn't witnessed the men following him, I probably would have thought his story was unlikely.

Johnnie was sitting and I stood with my back against the wall to the left of Marco's desk. Marco marched in carrying three glasses of my favorite bourbon.

He handed each of us a glass and pulled Skinny Vinnie to the chair next to Johnnie. "Sit down and drink," he commanded.

Vinnie dropped back into the seat like a limp sack of potatoes and slumped over. He finally sat up and said, "You all can protect me, right?"

Marco walked around to his seat. "Of course we can. But we need to know what we're protecting. So…what are we protecting here?"

Marco was careful not to tell Vinnie much of what was on his mind. He didn't want to talk about situations or mention names. He wanted to see what Vinnie knew without leading him.

Vinnie gulped down his drink in one swig and placed the glass on a small mahogany coffee table between the chairs.

"Oronzio wants me dead," he said. "and his attack dog, Marty Fucker. They know that I know. So they want me dead."

"You know what?" Johnnie asked.

"About Humpty…and the night he was murdered. It was a set-up. The whole fuckin' thing!"

Glances rolled between Marco, Johnnie, and I.

"Forgive me if I'm not completely sold on your information," Marco said. "How do you know for certain?"

"And how do we know that your extra-curricular activities haven't affected your ability to accurately recall events as they happened?" I said.

"Fuck you man! I've been clean for over a year. And I know what I saw!"

Now it was Marco's turn to sit straight up in his seat. "Saw? What did you see?"

"Mr. Ribisi, that's what I'm trying to tell you! That whole surveillance package Anthony set up with Humpty, it sure did come in handy."

Damn it! If my hunch was correct, Marco was thinking, *what surveillance package*? I looked at Marco but he never took his gaze off of Vinnie. "Go on," Marco said, without skipping a beat.

He didn't want Vinnie to think he was surprised about any facet of his organization. On top of that Marco hated having disagreements and arguments in front of outsiders. In his opinion, it showed a lack of discipline. He always told me that a family's dirty laundry should never be aired in the street.

"Well…" Vinnie continued, "Humpty brought me in to be his second man and monitor the video footage. Like I said, I've been clean for over a year, and I went to that technical college up in Beltsville, studying computers and electronics." He looked in my direction and added, "I upgraded that archaic shit you had. No offense."

"None taken," I replied.

"We were using a new hi-def video recorder with crystal clear night-vision, shooting in 1080p. And we installed a telescopic microphone that would pick up a penny hitting the floor from a hundred yards away. This let us to set up the camera and mic from a greater distance. We had a new email account and everything!"

"You don't say?" Marco said, eyes wide with sarcasm. But of course, it was directed at me and I think I was the only one who caught it.

"Two weeks before Humpty was murdered, we had a meet and greet with Oronzio. It was over in Rock Creek Park. Oronzio choose the place. It was in an empty parking lot. So of course we got there early, set up the equipment, then left."

"I remember," Marco said. "I sent him to that meeting." Marco turned to me and said, "Humpty was there to tell Oronzio about our exit plan. I wanted Oronzio to then inform the other bosses."

"Right. And that was pretty much how the meeting went. No surprises. Humpty gave him the message. Oronzio wasn't too pleased, but Humpty said that Oronzio didn't have much to say. So he bounced."

Marco leaned back with a frown, processing all of this.

"Anthony," Vinnie said speaking to me again. "so I left the equipment stashed like you taught Humpty to do. I was coming back to get it after the meeting."

I wished this guy would just get to the end of the story instead of digging a bigger hole for Marco to dump me in. With every reference to my surveillance strategy, I was certain Marco was planning a disciplinary course of action.

"Everything ticked like clockwork. When Humpty got home, he'd call to let me know he was safe, and then I'd head out to grab the equipment. And that's what he did. Humpty got home, we spoke for a few minutes, and it was all good.

"But after I got off the phone with him, this little shorty from school hit me up, asking me to come to her place. We had a test the next day and she wanted to see if I wanted to study. Come on now…she's calling at two in the morning. I knew what that meant. So I grabbed a few rubbers and headed over…to study."

"You didn't go back for the camera?" Johnnie asked.

"The way I looked at it," Vinnie said. "Humpty was safe at home. I didn't see the need to rush. And I had the fattest piece of ass waiting on me. I went back and grabbed the equipment, after leaving the chicks' place in the morning."

I shook my head but kept my mouth closed so that he could finish his story.

"Fast forward to the night of the murder," Vinnie said. "We hadn't had a meeting since the one with Oronzio, so there was no reason for me to go into the email inbox and fish out any videos, right...so I didn't touch it. But that night, I saw a commercial about a new video camera I wanted from Best Buy. And that's when it dawned on me that I never watched and deleted the video from the meeting."

At that point I interrupted him to sarcastically add, "Ticked like clockwork, huh? So far you left the equipment, and then forgot to watch and delete the video. Those parts are just as important as recording the meeting."

Vinnie scrunched his face and raised an eyebrow in annoyance. But he continued without directly addressing my comment. "Logging into the email account, I saw the email with the video from the meeting. But then guess what, genius," he finally said toward me. "I saw a second video attachment in different email. The time stamp was a little more than an hour after first."

"Another meeting?" Marco asked.

"Yes sir, Mr. Ribisi. There was a second meeting at the same place. The motion detector on the camera sensed movement and everything powered up. It was Marty Fucker. And he wasn't alone."

* * *

Marty parked a black SUV and climbed out. Leaning against the vehicle, he lit a cigarette and took a deep breath. Exhaling a cloud of smoke, he noticed a car carefully creeping toward him.

"It's about damn time," he said to himself.

He extinguished the ember at the tip of his cigarette on the heal of his shoe, and then nonchalantly tossed it to the ground. He stepped clear of the moving car, so as to give it enough space to pull close to him. The car coasted in, came to a stop, and then the engine died.

The driver didn't exit the car. Instead, Marty approached the passenger side window and tapped on it with a ring on his finger. The whirl of the window moving down filled the quiet night.

Marty inspected the car through the open window. "Ok. Just checking."

He looked back at his truck and made a signal. Oronzio climbed out. By the time he reached the car, Marty had already moved to the back passenger side door and had it open, waiting for Oronzio.

Once Oronzio was inside, Marty closed the door and stepped back to truck. The window of the car was rolled up again. The vehicle had been sealed. Marty couldn't hear the conversation inside. But he didn't need to. He already knew the topic of discussion. After ten minutes, Oronzio exited the car, closed the door and walked back to Marty.

The car reversed out of its parking space a lot faster than it had pulled in, leaving Marty and Oronzio alone in the parking lot.

"Is everything set?" Marty asked.

Oronzio was in thought. His face was stoic. His demeanor, rigid. "Who the hell does he think he is?" he asked. "We are not involved with something that can be dropped whenever he fucking feels like it. If he wants to leave, it won't be on his terms. There's too much at stake for that to happen. We'll have to crush him. His whole operation. Break it up piece by piece, until there's nothing left. Then the gambling game will be mine. If he wants to leave, it'll have to be in a box."

Marty cracked a smile. "So then everything is in place. That's good to hear. Piece by piece, you say?"

"By motherfucking piece. And where do we start?" It was a rhetorical question, but Marty knew that. "We start with the errand boy."

"He won't know what hit him," Marty said.

It was Oronzio's turn to smile. "Not until it's too late."

* * *

"Talk about killing the messenger!" Vinnie said. "I couldn't hear what was going on in the car, but it was clear they were talking about you, Mr. Ribisi. They wanted to put a fork in you and were going to start by killing Humpty.

"I had no idea of their timeline, so I hopped on the phone and called Humpty, but he didn't answer. The first two times I called, he sent it to voicemail. The third time, it rang until the voicemail picked up. I didn't know if I was too late."

"Vinnie, we saw the video from the night of the murder," Johnnie said. "How come you didn't get it?"

"Humpty must have gone with the old system and set it up alone. Which probably means that video went to the old email address. I tried to reach him. Man, I swear I did."

Marco cleared his throat, so as to get everyone's attention. "Vinnie, let me ask you, you wouldn't still have that video, would you?"

"I deleted it from the email, Mr. Ribisi. But I saved a copy to my laptop."

"Good boy," he said to Vinnie. Then he looked at me. "We need that computer. ASAP."

"Yes, sir."

"Alright gentleman, this is what's going to happen..." Marco began. But he couldn't finish his statement before Johnnie's phone started ringing. He looked at him like, "*Turn your phone off.*" But before he could get the words out, my phone started ringing. Then Marco's cell phone joined in a chorus.

We looked at each other with the feeling that this wasn't coincidental. And when Marco's desk phone began ringing off the hook, we were certain of it. We let our cell phones ring and waited for Marco to pick up his office phone.

"This is Ribisi." He listened intently to the person on the other end. Before he hung up, he said. "We'll be right there."

Once he hung up, he opened his desk drawer, took his gun out of its holster, tossed it in the drawer and slammed it shut.

"If you two are armed," he said, "leave your guns here. We need to get to House number two. It's crawling with cops and firefighters. Apparently, there was a gas explosion."

Johnnie and I looked at each other in disbelief. House number two was the first house Marco had shut down. Gas explosion? How?

It had been empty for months.

Chapter 33

We decided to take separate cars. Johnnie chauffeured Marco in his father's vehicle and Vinnie rode with me. He made a ruckus about being left alone at the restaurant. I tried to convince him that he'd be safer there, but Vinnie wasn't buying it and wanted to be with us.

The ride to the house was quiet, for the most part. Just the way I like my car rides. It gave me quality time with my own thoughts. Between sitting silently at stoplights and the humming tires rolling against the asphalt, Vinnie must have felt uncomfortable.

"Turn on some tunes, man." He didn't wait for me to answer. Instead he leaned forward and hit the power button on the stereo and started turning the volume dial. I switched it off. "Hey! What gives?"

I said, "No radio." Without looking at him.

Vinnie slammed himself back into his seat. He eyed the old school cassette deck and said, "At least you got some tapes in here, or something man?"

This time, I didn't respond. He fidgeted around for a little bit, growing even more uncomfortable, I assumed. There was nothing left for him to do, other than stare out the window. He settled on doing just that.

"Can I ask you a question?" he mumbled out.

Certain he would ask anyway I said, "Mmm hmm."

"What's the deal with you and Marco? How'd you end up working for him?"

We were still a few minutes from the house and since I said he could ask me a question, I felt it wouldn't hurt to give him an answer. But of course, I weighed how transparent I would be. I choose opaque.

"He needed help at the restaurant. I needed a job." I said, sitting at another red light. I knew that non-answer wasn't what he was looking for.

Vinnie looked at me. And even though I wasn't looking at him, I could sense the seriousness in his face. "That's not what I mean. I can tell he trusts you." He turned and looked out the window again, at the passing streetlamps. "I don't know if anyone's trusted me like he trusts you." After a pause he said, "Well, my cousin trusted me. And look where that got him."

"The guy at your house with the same tattoo. That was your cousin?" That explained why the dead guy was so similar to Skinny, and it also meant Oronzio didn't know Skinny was still alive.

Vinnie looked straight ahead. "When I hadn't heard from you or Johnnie, I packed a bag and left. I didn't wanna risk getting on the public bus or train so I took my grandma's old Honda that she had stashed behind the house. I was sure it would get me to the train station, but not much farther.

"Soon as I hit the corner and made it down the block, I saw David coming up the street. I was gonna call out to him. Try to stop him from going to the house. But then I saw a man about ten feet behind. It looked like he was following him. I was scared. I froze up, and he walked into the house. Right after David.

"The tattoo...four of the cousins have it. The family moved to DC from New Orleans, when my mother was a child. And the compass points us in the right direction whenever we're lost. The fleur-de-lis is supposed to help us remember our roots. I used to have a safe place to go. I don't anymore."

And just then, I got it. His grandmother's house was a safe haven for not just him, but his cousins as well. It was the home that anchored them together. That was a place where they would always feel secure and protected.

I wanted to console him, even if it was a small attempt. "Don't beat yourself up," I said. "We're all trusting you tonight. After checking out the fire damage, we'll get that laptop, and once we have the proof we need, we'll address Oronzio. A bullet in him can bring you safety."

"Safe. Really?" he asked, looking up ahead.

We had rolled to a stop two blocks away from what could only be described as a raging inferno. Marco and Johnnie were waiting for us outside of their car.

I didn't want Vinnie to think I was blowing smoke up his behind, but it was too late. He didn't believe me.

All I could do was look at him. It was the first time I turned my head in his direction, the entire car ride.

I didn't say a word. I only reached for the handle and left him in the car. I walked toward Marco and Johnnie, but could see Vinnie over my shoulder. He hadn't moved yet. He was too busy wiping the tears from his eyes.

Chapter 34

House number two was on Seaton Place, on the Northwest side of North Capitol Street. It was a red brick row home that was perfectly situated between two abandon row homes. Without people on either side, there was never a problem with disturbing sleeping neighbors.

The location of the house was a pretty good one for us. Being between two abandoned homes made its location great for loud noises and gambling, but horrible with regards to the fire. It appeared that the fire started at our house but quickly jumped to the abandoned properties, making the flames stronger and more difficult to fight.

As we ran the two blocks to the commotion, the roar from amber and yellow flames grew louder. The all-consuming flames reached skyward. I counted four fire engines and two trucks with ladders extended as high as they could go. Water spray from the countless hoses flew into our faces.

Careful not to get too close to the action, we stopped at the first set of cop cars that blocked off traffic at First Street and Seaton Place. A small crowd of neighborhood residents came out to see the show too.

We really just wanted to have a watchful eye on the activities. The plan was to let them put the fire out and then lay low until everyone left. But we came with no idea of how ferocious the blaze actually was. They didn't look anywhere close to getting it under control. The fire had quickly spread to the adjacent row homes.

"You don't plan on being here all night?" Johnnie asked his father.

Marco squinted toward the middle of the block, where all the action was happening. "Hmm?" He was so focused that he hadn't heard his son.

"Pop?" Johnnie said, trying to get Marco's attention. "This is gonna go on all night."

Marco shook himself from his trance, looked at me and then faced Johnnie. "You're right. You all get out of here and find that laptop. I want to see if there's anything here that can lead back to Oronzio. I can't think of anyone else who'd be behind this."

"You can't possibly see any need in staying?" Johnnie protested. "There's nothing for you to do here. Plus it's just not safe!"

Marco didn't respond, so Johnnie continued. "Anthony. Talk some sense into this man."

"Johnnie has a point," I quickly said. "There's no need to make a marathon night of this. All we need is Vinnie's laptop. You should go back to the restaurant or home. Like Johnnie said, it's not safe."

Marco fixed his eyes on the house that was being reduced to ashes. He reluctantly shook his head. "You're right, Johnnie. Let's go. We have work to do."

There was a look of agreement between everyone. Marco would go home. And then Vinnie, Johnnie and I would fetch Vinnie's laptop.

"You've got to be kidding me about it not being safe," Marco said. He wrapped his arms around Jonnie's shoulders. "With all these cops, it's gotta be the safest place in DC right now."

Marco laughed and then started walking back to the cars. Even in the middle of everything that was going on, we found a moment of lighthearted agreement. But that was shattered and turned into confusion and chaos quickly.

Our attention was caught by the eruption of glass. Everything stopped. We looked at each other, confused. The window of a nearby squad car exploded. We were being shot at!

The four of us jumped to the ground. There were more shots and glass was everywhere.

* * *

Flashes of light came from the direction of our parked cars, at least three stories above the ground. Whoever was shooting was perched on the roof of one of the row homes. Bullets ripped though the squad car, just above my head. I could feel the air splitting.

Some of the fire watching crowd ran for cover while others scurried into their homes. The uproar alerted the police on scene to the hail of bullets flying in our direction. The rampage of the fire, sirens, and at this point, collapsing building structures, made it impossible for the police to hear the initial shots.

But by this time, they were on their way in our direction. Guns drawn. I noticed that the shots stopped as soon as the cops responded.

I picked my head fully off the ground for the first time. I tried to survey the area and see the result of the mayhem. There was a puddle of blood on my right, between my body, and the squad car. I immediately started moving and feeling for bullet wounds. I wasn't experiencing any pain so I knew I hadn't been shot.

Pulling myself up on one knee, I twisted my torso completely around to see Skinny Vinnie. He was right behind me. His back was against the squad car and slightly slumped to his left.

The puddle came from two obvious bullet wounds. One shot ripped through his neck and it was still spewing out blood. The second and more gruesome wound was a gaping hole on the right side of his face. A bullet had torn open his skull.

I promised to keep him safe and here he was dead, minutes later. We'd walked right into a trap. We'd been playing into their hands all along.

It had felt like we were getting a handle on our situation and just like that...another dead body. Uncovering the specifics of Humpty's murder was proving to be more and more difficult. I was becoming concerned that we'd never find the truth. Clearly there were forces working to keep us in the dark and it looked like they were going to win.

Police and emergency medical technicians pushed me away from the car so they had space to work on Vinnie, but it was too late. He was dead. If not, he certainly would die within seconds. No one would be able to survive the injuries he sustained.

I looked around for Marco and Johnnie and couldn't see them...at first. But all it took was for me to follow the second set of EMTs over to the only other two men on the street. They were between two parked cars. One was lying on his back, head toward the curb and legs extended out into the street, while the other was on his knees and bent over him.

I found them. Johnnie was kneeling over his father with his hands over a single bullet hole that entered Marco's chest. He was applying pressure in the hopes to stymie the blood flowing out of Marco's body. Blood still leaked out and there was now a steady flow steaming down onto the asphalt.

Johnnie had tears in his eyes as the EMTs reached him. "Pop!" he called out. The emergency personnel had to fight to pry Johnnie away from Marco. "Pop!" he cried out as he was being dragged away.

Marco wanted to leave the life of illegal gambling behind, but I was sure it wasn't like this. I was sure of another thing as well. Someone knew we were getting close and they didn't like it. House number two must have been intentionally set on fire to lure Marco out and kill him.

Killing Vinnie was probably icing on the cake.

Chapter 35

He didn't have time to disassemble the rifle and put it back in its case. He was already behind schedule. So he grabbed the case's handle and made his way to the extension ladder that was leaned against the back of the abandoned row house.

He let go of the gun case and watched it fall three stories to the grass below. With the rifle slung over his shoulder he climbed down the metal ladder, rung by rung, until he reached the ground.

He required a little help getting out of the situation he found himself in at Union Station. The inside man from Metropolitan Police Department arrived to escort him to the police station as a suspect in custody. But all he really did was drive him to his truck that was parked in an alley off of the dark and secluded First Street.

While he moved swiftly, he showed no signs of anxiety. After picking up the case, he walked around to the front of the house and hopped in the waiting Ford Excursion with tinted windows. The engine was already running. Baldie sat behind the wheel.

Navy blue suit guy settled in the passenger seat. "It's done."

"Both of them?"

"Mmm hmm."

That's all Baldie needed to hear. The truck made a u-turn and drove off in the opposite direction of the fire. By the time the first officer arrived, they were gone.

Chapter 36

Marco was out of surgery. I stood by while Johnnie sat at his father's bedside. He leaned over with his head resting on the bedrail. His sobs simmered to a quiet weep. We had no idea what was going on with Marco.

Nick Nick had arrived at the hospital. I met him at the door.

"Did you get his wallet?" he asked.

I nodded.

"Name?" he continued.

"Jones," I said. "It was the first that came to mind."

"That's good."

We didn't want word getting out that Marco was here and alive. I used the *fake* name to keep it quiet.

"My guess is that with all the commotion surrounding the fire, the shooter didn't stick around to see if he got a kill shot. It may be assumed that Marco is dead. That's what he'll probably tell Oronzio."

"And if I know Oronzio," Nick Nick interrupted, "he'll probably keep his mouth shut and play dumb. Any prior knowledge of this would implicate him."

"What about everyone else?" I asked.

"Nobody needs to know anything. At least, not for now."

I looked at Marco and my body trembled. Slight tremors that no one could see. But they were there. There was too much to do and I couldn't give in to the pain I was feeling. Not yet.

Dr. Adenuga walked in a minute after Nick Nick. He was Marco's surgeon. Dr. Adenuga scribbled some notes on Marco's chart and then placed the clipboard in a Plexiglas box at the foot of the bed. Recognizing that Johnnie was in no position to have a discussion, he walked back to Nick Nick and me.

Dr. Adenuga addressed us both. "Mr. Jones' bullet wound is taken care of. The bleeding has been stopped and there isn't major internal damage that we need to worry about."

"That's a good thing, right?" Nick Nick said optimistically.

"It would've been, if that was his only injury," Dr. Adenuga said. "His head slammed against the back of his skull when he hit the ground and now there is intracranial pressure."

"What does that mean?" Johnnie said softly. He didn't move or look in our direction. He only wiped tears from his face.

"It means that his brain is swollen. And as a result, the metabolism of the brain has been significantly altered, you understand? There are certain actions the brain needs to undertake in order for it to function properly, but because of the injury it can't. It won't have the necessary blood flow. So in effect, what we had to do was reduce the amount of energy the brain needs to work."

"What does that mean, Doc?" Johnnie said more forceful than before.

"Mr. Jones. We had to place your father in a coma. The brain needs to conserve its energy, which will allow the swelling to go down."

Johnnie chuckled to himself. "So he survives the bullet, but might lose out to the bump on the head. Ain't this a bitch?" he said to no one specifically.

"A coma!" Nick Nick said. "For how long?"

"That's hard to tell. It could be six days or six months. It all depends on when the swelling goes down. If it happens quickly, then I'll ease him off the barbiturates, which will let his body take over and then he'll heal on his own."

Dr. Adenuga's pager beeped as soon as he put a period at the end of his sentence. Once he checked it, he excused himself to look in on another patient. There wasn't any more he could tell us, so we were fine with him leaving. He was sure to shut the door on his way out.

The room fell silent. Nick Nick joined Johnnie at the bed. "He's strong Johnnie. He'll make it."

For the moment, Johnnie had no words. Typically he was a whirlwind of emotions, so I just stood back and waited for it. Right now, he was somber...in pain over the condition of his father, but I knew anger was on its way.

And it made its presence known in a fashion more subdued than I anticipated. "I'm gonna kill him," Johnnie said with an even tone.

Nick Nick looked at Johnnie and placed his hand on his shoulder. Johnnie shook it off. "We know this was Oronzio. And I'm going to kill him."

"Let's think about this. Now isn't the time to do anything hurried or impatient."

"Fuck him!" Johnnie shot back. The lava was beginning to bubble to the top.

"I think we should listen to Nick Nick. We have a plan," I said.

"With my father lying here like a damn vegetable? No! Fuck focus! Oronzio dies. Tonight!"

The door to the hospital slowly crept open. Jena poked her head in to make sure she had the right room. After a look around, she ran past me and headed straight for her twin brother.

"Johnnie! I got here as soon as I could. How's Pop?" she asked between the sobs and hugs.

"He's not good, sis. Go ahead and spend a little time with him. I've gotta go." Johnnie kissed Jena on her forehead. He then stepped away from the door and approached me. "This ain't the time for focus or patience. These fuckers are laughing at us. All of this for the houses, that he was shutting down anyway? You can sit this one out if you want, Anthony. I'm going to do something about it. And it would really be nice if you acted like you gave a fuck!"

Nick Nick walked over and interrupted. "Johnnie. Is that necessary?"

Johnnie looked me in my eyes. "My father loves you. Like he loves me and Jena. They put a bullet in him and you don't even shed a fuckin' tear!"

I didn't say a word. I could see the volcano was erupting. Johnnie was beyond angry and there would have been no reasoning with him. So I just let him talk.

"With or without you two…and don't try to stop me."

Johnnie stormed out of the room.

"I'm sorry about this, Anthony," Nick Nick said. "Look after Jena. I'll go talk some sense into the boy." He pulled me close and whispered. "At least for tonight...don't let her out of your sight."

I acknowledged Nick Nick's command with the nod of my head. Then he quickly walked out the room in pursuit of Johnnie. Jena had spent this time in silence by her father's side. She was so consumed with what was going on with Marco that she hadn't heard a word of my conversation with Nick Nick and Johnnie.

I didn't rush her. I'd stay all night, if that's what she needed. I just spent that time thinking about what Johnnie said. *"And it would really be nice if you acted like you gave a fuck!"*

Those words echoed in my mind. I couldn't understand exactly how Johnnie wanted me to act. He was a mess, so someone had to hold it together.

Other than his kids, no one's love for Marco could match mine. But that didn't change anything. Just as with Humpty's death, if I were going to address the situation, I would need to keep a clear head. And sooner or later, Johnnie would appreciate my even keeled way of reasoning through dilemmas and tragedy.

At least, that's what I was hoping.

Chapter 37

As soon as we walked into my apartment, Jena dropped her duffle bag on the floor. "You sure you don't mind?" she asked.

"For the tenth time. My crib is your crib. Being at your place probably isn't the best or safest idea anyway."

"What? I'm better protected here?" She unsuccessfully tried to joke to herself. "You know, as many times as I've met you outside, I've never been *in* your place, much less stayed the night." Jena spoke while making her observations around the living room.

"It's ok. Everyone's allowed to make a mistake. I won't hold it against you."

And for the first time Jena's facial expression read something other than pain. She narrowed her eyes, pursed her lips and then said, "Maaaaan, whatever!"

Jena made her way back to me and did the only thing that felt natural in that moment. She wrapped her arms around my waist and pressed the side of her cheek against my chest. She squeezed hard and I squeezed back.

I couldn't imagine what she was going through. Marco meant the world to her. And the loss of her father would leave her devastated. So I let her squeeze. Not soon after, I felt wetness on my shirt, and I let her cry.

* * *

It took about fifteen minutes before Jena calmed down enough to get ready for bed. She had showered and changed into pink and white flannel pajamas. Her dark hair was pulled away from her face and held together in a ponytail.

Jena walked between me and television, and headed straight for the kitchen. Even though I've watched it more than a dozen times, *Swimming with Sharks* was in the DVD player. I heard the refrigerator door open.

"Who the hell drinks this Corona shit?" Jena yelled.

I didn't bother responding.

"Well, if this is all you have," she conceded, walking toward me with a bottle in hand, "then I guess."

"Some people actually like Corona."

"Yeah? Like who? Because I know you don't drink this."

Jena waited for me to respond, but I didn't say anything.

"Ohhh," she dragged out. "Must belong to the girlfriend. Who knew you had a lady?" Jena dropped onto the sofa, next to me with her legs and feet curled up underneath her body.

"If you wanna know whether I have a girl or not, why don't you just ask?" I said. That's when she leaned her head against my shoulder.

"I couldn't care less."

"Whatever you say."

My nonchalance had brought the discussion to a close and I continued to watch my movie.

I tried to be mindful of Jena's state of mind, but in truth, I was exhausted and I knew she was as well. Her eyes were closed and her head was nodding.

She reminded me of a toddler fighting sleep before taking a nap. I thought it was a perfect time to move her into the bedroom. It had been a long and rough day. I was ready to pass out on the sofa, myself.

"Ok, little lady. It's time to hop in the bed."

Her eyes fluttered open. I helped her up by her waist. We took slow steps toward the portal of my bedroom.

"I'm sleeping in your bed?" she asked.

"Mmm Hmm."

"You?"

"I have a pillow and blanket for the sofa. Get some rest. I'll be right out here." I let go of Jena's waist and backed away from her.

She wasn't having it.

Jena extended her hand and balled a fistful of my t-shirt within it.

"What? No goodnight kiss?" And without waiting for a reply, she pulled me closer. Or shall I say, I allowed her to pull me closer. I could have resisted.

Unsure of what was about to happen, I didn't make any sudden moves. Was this woman about to kiss me? There had always been a little flirtation between the two of us, but nothing had ever become physical. Come to think of it, outside of a hug every now and then, we had never stood so close. And not for a prolonged period of time.

Jena took her free hand and held the back of my head. She stood taller on her toes and brought me even closer.

She rubbed her cheek against mine and angled her mouth toward the corner my lips. Then she kissed me.

Drunk off of pheromones and the excitement of the moment, I didn't know if her mouth was open or closed. I couldn't tell. But I didn't want the craziness of the night to cause us to do anything that we would regret. So I backed away just a few inches and looked at her.

That's when she pulled me in again. And this time she gave me a real kiss. Squarely on the mouth. This time, her mouth was agape. Her tongue began to massage my lips. She pushed her tongue into my mouth and I didn't stop her.

It felt good and I felt bad. Even though Coco and I hadn't made any concrete moves toward being a couple, the potential of it happening was enough to make me feel guilty. But I still didn't stop Jena.

It wasn't until she took my hand and slid it in between the buttons of her pajama top that I caught myself. Here I was groping and kissing a woman that I considered to be like a sister. And the most important thought was that this was all happening at a vulnerable time for her. But maybe the closeness was what she needed to get through the night.

"Hold up..." I interrupted. "Things are getting a little out of control. I think we need to go to bed."

"Then let's go to bed," she said, attempting to pull me into the bedroom.

"Jena," I said in protest.

"Don't act like you haven't wanted to." I couldn't even deny that assertion. "If this day has taught us anything," she continued, "...it's that tomorrow isn't guaranteed. So if we have tonight, then Anthony, let's have tonight."

Her words were absolutely correct. Marco had been shot, and lying in a coma with the potential of death. That changed everything. What we knew about our future had just been turned upside-down. The certainty of security was no longer a luxury we could afford. At least not without taking control and exercising our own will.

It had been made clearer; Johnnie, Jena, and I were becoming more responsible for our here and now. And more importantly, responsible for our future.

I could tell she noticed the look on my face changing from one of protest to one of agreement. I took a step closer and Jena knew I was ready.

"Besides..." she said "I could've sworn I heard Nick Nick tell you not to let me out of your sight."

My response to her was, "Well, he did. At least for tonight."

Chapter 38

I never had a problem with walking to the restaurant. I enjoyed the time alone. Especially when I had to think through things. And boy, were there some things to think about. Like Jena, for example.

But the bigger issue was the attempt on Marco's life. He was stashed away at the hospital under an alias. I was still worried about the old man, but for the moment, he was safe.

We all agreed to carry on with our daily activities, as if all was well. We didn't want anyone else to know that Marco had been shot and was in the hospital. So we'd continue as if everything was good, but we knew it wasn't.

Since consistency was the plan, Jena needed to be at the restaurant a couple hours early, to prepare and organize the bar. I didn't leave with her, but I was still concerned for her safety. I gave her my car keys and told her that I would walk. That way, her travel time was cut from a twenty-minute walk to a five-minute drive. I lived on Columbia Road, in the Columbia Heights neighborhood, so getting to the restaurant was never a problem.

Jena called to let me know she made it without incident. That put me at ease. We had a small security team waiting and then there was Nick Nick. He was practically a one-man security team. His presence, alone, ensured Jena's safety.

By the time I made my way down the street, I had thought about our night together a few different times. Or maybe it was one continuous line of thinking that was interrupted by thoughts of Coco. At the same time, I felt both euphoric and guilty.

On one hand, there was Jena who seemed ready and able to be close with me. While on the other hand, Coco made it clear that she wasn't. I knew that the unanswered questions about who I was and what I did presented problems for Coco. But with Jena, she was there the whole time. There were no questions. She knew who I was and what I did for her father. If one could accept it and act solely on how she felt for me, why couldn't the other?

And that's what I wanted. The other. I wanted Coco and I wanted her to accept me the way I was.

Then there was the other problem. Jena was a Ribisi. I worked for her father, and he thought of me as his own son. I couldn't imagine what his response would be if he knew I slept with his daughter. But I was pretty sure how Johnnie would respond. He wouldn't like it at all.

I had so much on my mind. What would I do about Jena? How did our night together affect what was going on with me and Coco? Would it be smarter to leave the both of them alone? And as for Johnnie, I just didn't have enough left over brain power to think about him and his reaction.

Something caught my attention suddenly. With all that was running through my mind, I couldn't tell how long the black SUV had been following me. The windows were tinted, so I didn't know who was inside, but I was sure it followed me the entire time I walked down Sixteenth Street.

To be certain, I crossed the street at the stoplight. This put me on the opposite side of the road. I was now on the sidewalk bordering Meridian Hill Park. The SUV was sitting at the red light. The driver's side window came down a few inches and for the first time I was able to make out a white man with dark brown eyes, staring across the street at me as I walked a measured pace.

I really wasn't in the mood to find out who he was and what he wanted. But looking into his eyes, I could tell he knew what I was about to do. It was time to see how committed he was to tailing with me.

I changed direction and ran up the stairs leading into the park. The black vehicle was still stuck at the red light, but the brown-eyed driver didn't care. He drove into the intersection. Oncoming cars slammed on their brakes and swerved out the way to avoid hitting him.

The SUV made a U-turn, at full speed. And without the vehicle coming to a complete stop, a dark haired white man, in a dark suit, jumped out of the passenger seat and began hoping the park stairs, two at a time. The truck peeled off and accelerated north.

Before the man on foot could catch up to me, I was already headed south into the park and making my way toward Fifteenth Street. I felt like that was a good strategy. I knew I could outrun the man chasing me. And since the truck headed north, the only way they'd be able to catch me would be if they drove south on Fifteenth Street, which was one-way going north.

I exited the park, thinking to myself that they wouldn't be that crazy. I looked back and didn't see the guy chasing me, so I took a minute to catch my breath and then began to briskly walk south toward W Street. Until I heard honking and yelling. They were, in fact, crazy. I spotted the huge SUV barreling southbound on a northbound one-way street. It was driving with determination in a straight line.

I found myself running as fast as I could, recognizing that they were catching up. All I wanted to do was get to Fifteenth and W. That particular intersection was the meeting point for five separate streets. There was no way they'd be able to get through it without hitting at least one other vehicle.

Just a few feet away from Fifteenth and W, I saw the truck was approximately twenty feet behind. I reached the intersection, but had to give it a second to let two cars pass through. It didn't make any sense for me to get hit.

As the last car cleared the street, I stepped off of the curb. Home free, I thought. Only to be grabbed from behind—by the dark hair, dark suit man.

I fought back but couldn't shake him. The SUV came to a screeching halt before entering the intersection. The timing couldn't have been better for them, or worse for me. They were inches away from t-boning the car I was waiting to clear the intersection.

The back passenger window was down. Oronzio appeared, his face was red and his eyes bulged with anger. He placed an arm in the window and leaned in my direction.

"Get the fuck in the truck."

Chapter 39

I sat in the back seat with Oronzio. His guys sat up front. Oronzio's face was still flushed. I guess riding against traffic down a one-way street didn't sit too well with him. He appeared to be trying to calm himself before initiating a conversation.

He shook his head and waved a hand at me. "Oh, relax!" he finally said. "If I wanted you dead, it would've happened back at your building. Besides, you're not the one that almost ended up wrapped around a light pole!"

Relaxing, just because he said so, wasn't going to happen. I looked out of the heavily tinted window to get a glimpse of where we were headed. Out to the Catoctin Mountains of Maryland, perhaps? Or did he already have a hole dug for me in the suburbs of Woodbridge, VA? Oronzio didn't seem like a Southeast DC kind of guy, so I didn't imagine us heading to the Anacostia River. There are way too many black people out there for white folks to inconspicuously dump a black body.

Where were we going? It was driving me crazy until I noticed that we had passed my block for a second time. I started to relax, not because Oronzio asked me to, but because it was clear that we were driving in circles.

Oronzio finally spoke. "Anthony, you need to tell Nick Nick that it wasn't me."

"Pardon me?" I said.

"This fuckin' guy. I'm talking about Marco. I didn't order the hit!"

Ordinarily, I have an excellent poker face, a skill I picked up over the years, but something about my demeanor must have shown exactly what was on my mind. *How in the hell did he know Marco was alive?*

"Come on," he continued. "You think your outfit is the only one with inside guys? We can get info too, you know. That little 'Mr. Jones' trick might work on paramedics and doctors, but not me.

"I'll let y'all keep your little secret, but I knew what hospital room Marco was in before you did. And I only share this because I need you to know and believe me. I had nothing to do with him getting shot."

"Why should I believe you?"

"You're not looking at the bigger picture," Oronzio said in a frustrated tone. "There are others who have just as much to gain with Marco out of the way. Don't believe me?" He chuckled to himself. "Then ask Nick Nick. He knows."

I felt the SUV pull over to the curb, double-parking for the moment. I looked up to see that I was a block away from the restaurant.

"This is where you were going, right? I would take you to the front door, but I'd rather you smooth things over before I show my face anywhere near here."

I reached for the car door to let myself out. "I can't make any promises."

Once outside of the truck, I looked back at the window and Oronzio rolled it down. "Why would anyone go through the trouble of setting you up?" I asked.

"For the same reason anyone does anything in this town," he replied in a tired voice. "Whether in the hood or on the Hill. It's all about power."

Chapter 40

When I walked into the restaurant, Smitty was there and entering Marco's office. I hadn't seen him since Johnnie and I were at Red Lounge. He turned his head to look over his shoulder and pointed into the office, clearly indicating to me that I was walking straight into a meeting.

Jena was at the bar making her usual preparations for the evening's opening. I took a couple steps toward Marco's office, and then changing my mind, I doubled back to Jena. She stopped what she was doing and walked toward me once I approached the bar.

"How you doing?" I asked. "You ok?"

She shrugged. "Ah. As good as I'm gonna be."

"What about us? Are we good?"

She gave the same shrug. "Don't worry, Anthony. I'm a big girl. I knew what I was doing. Besides, you have your little girlfriend."

"It's not like that."

"Well, whatever it is, what's done is done. We can leave it at that." She leaned over the bar and gave me a light kiss on my lips. I felt a little apprehensive but let it slide because I knew everyone was in the office and I was sure they couldn't see through walls. "Unless you want a Round Two," she continued, "Oh, I'm sorry. Round Three, since we technically had Round Two this morning."

At that moment, Nick Nick called for me. "Anthony!"

"Look at that," I said with a smile. "Saved by the yell."

Chapter 41

"Guess who wanted to carpool me to the office today?" I said aloud as I walked in.

"Please don't tell me he was fool enough," Nick Nick said. He was sitting behind Marco's desk.

Smitty was standing at the door, with an eye out into the restaurant. *Shit!* Maybe he *had* seen Jena and I. If he had, he didn't let on.

"I wish I could say that he wasn't, but he was."

"I'm shocked he didn't just kill you," Smitty added from behind me.

"That's the interesting thing. He just wanted to talk."

"Really?" Nick Nick was puzzled. "Well, what did he want?"

"He knows about Marco. And he says it wasn't him."

Smitty walked closer to us and Nick Nick got up out of his seat.

"What? This isn't good." Nick Nick said.

"If he knows..." Smitty added. "Then who the hell else knows?"

"I think he's the only one. He said he'd keep it to himself. So in my view, the party I'm planning for Friday is still on. I don't think there's a reason to worry.

Everything should go as planned; we just need to hammer out the specifics."

"Between me, you and Johnnie, do we have enough people?" Smitty asked.

"We need you here, watching over the restaurant. All hell will break loose come Friday night and a little protection at the home base wouldn't hurt. Johnnie and I can handle the party." I said.

"If you think you're leaving me out of this one Anthony, think again. You and Johnnie won't be doing this one alone," Nick Nick interjected.

Smitty took a ceremonious look around the office and asked, "Speaking of Johnnie, where is he?"

And Smitty was right for asking. Johnnie knew we had the meeting set to discuss the plans for the party and should've been at the restaurant long before I got there. Especially since Oronzio had held me up.

"He had calmed down yesterday and said that he would meet you at your place, before coming here." Nick Nick pointed at me.

Everyone was silent and looking at each other. Nick Nick spoke up again, but this time his frustration came through.

"So nobody knows where this boy is?!"

It didn't take long before it made sense. I looked at my watch and noticed the time. "Damn it!" I said. "I know exactly where he is."

Chapter 42

Johnnie had been waiting patiently in his car, at the corner of Fourteenth and V Streets, for well over two hours. The all black, twenty-one ounce Smith and Wesson Model 386 revolver sat in his lap.

He kept his eyes on the front door of Red Lounge. But at the same time, he was focused enough to inspect the number of bullets that were in the six-shooter. *Six is more than enough*, he thought to himself. One for each bodyguard, if they got in his way, and one for Marty Fucker.

After hitting Marty, he decided he'd make his way across town to find Oronzio. This was the night they all would pay. Anyone who had anything to do with the attempt on his father's life was subject to his wrath.

His phone rang. "Anthony" flashed across his screen. He ignored it.

After sitting in his car for another five minutes, the phone rang again. This time "Nick Nick" came across the screen. Giving it more consideration, he decided to answer it.

"What?" Johnnie calmly said.

"Where are you buddy?" Nick Nick asked.

"Handling business real quick."

"We have business back here at the restaurant too. You think you can get on over here?"

That's when Johnnie saw Marty walk out of Red Lounge.

"Can't talk right now. Gotta go," Johnnie said before hanging up the phone.

Johnnie dropped his phone in between the driver and passenger seats. He then jumped out of the car and slid the revolver into his right jacket pocket. He kept Marty in his sights from a block away. The one thing that made Johnnie feel more comfortable about his decision was that he didn't see any bodyguards. When Marty left the club, he had a pretty young lady with him, but that was it.

Johnnie began to walk faster in order to get closer to Marty. He was weaving through the crowd of late night partygoers. With regards to people on the street, Thursday night was no different than Friday or Saturday on U Street. The overflowing streets buzzed with electricity.

By the time Marty crossed U Street, walking south on Fourteenth, Johnnie was approximately twenty feet behind him. This was perfect, Johnnie thought.

Marty was swaying side to side and it almost looked like his female companion was doing her best to hold him up. Marty was tipsy at least, and full out drunk at most. This increased the chances that Johnnie would be able to complete his hit on him.

Ten feet away. Johnnie was closing in. He reached into his jacket pocket and retrieved the black revolver. He dropped his hand down to his side. Since he was wearing black denim, the gun was camouflaged and no one noticed it.

Five feet away. This was close enough for Johnnie. He raised the gun and leveled it to the back of Marty's head. And now he was three feet away. Fully conscious of what he was about to do. It somewhat shocked him that he was holding a gun three feet away from someone's head and no one was paying attention.

Johnnie's index finger was wrapped around the trigger of the gun. He gave it a tug. Never having fired this gun before, he felt a slight resistance. He regripped the firearm and prepared to send the fatal shot to the back of Marty Fucker's skull.

But it was too good to be true. Someone yanked him into the alley he passed with enough force to give him whiplash. The only thing Johnnie could think was, "*Fucking bodyguards*!"

* * *

It was at that moment that Marty's sixth sense kicked in. The alcohol must have dulled it for the time he walked down the street. But something urged him to turn around. Begged him even. He looked back because he had a feeling that he was being followed. But when he turned around he didn't see anything that would cause him to be alarmed.

Marty kept on his same track. Never knowing how close he came to a bullet in the back of his head.

Chapter 43

There was always a relaxing calm before the restaurant opened for the evening. Waitstaff shuffled back and forth, setting up tables and making sure everything was in order.

Jena was at her normal station, with her back leaned against the inside of the bar, staring out into space. She'd been there for a couple hours and had the bar set, prepped and ready to go.

It was quiet and Jena couldn't help but mull over everything that recently happened. The attempted assassination of her father and sleeping with Anthony weighed heavily on her mind. But of course, the former was more of a concern than the latter.

Thinking about her night with Anthony wasn't a burden, but more a source of stress release. For the time Jena was with him, she wasn't concerned about her safety or preoccupied with the fear of losing her father.

For those brief moments, she enjoyed having an intimate experience with a person she cared for deeply. She had always loved him. And although she said she loved him "like a brother" she knew that wasn't entirely true.

The love Jena extended to him was unconditional, but she would be fooling herself if she said it was solely platonic. Though she never shared it with anyone, she had been physically attracted to Anthony ever since they were in their late teenage years.

So their night and morning together was a long awaited fantasy, which is why thinking about it wasn't a burden. Dealing with the thoughts of her father, on the other hand, was tearing her apart.

The possibility of her father's death was a lot to deal with. And what complicated the matter was that she had to, at least up until this point, act as if everything was regular. And life was anything but regular.

Those were the thoughts that kept her mind spinning. So much so that she didn't notice Coco, who had walked in through the front door. It was only moments before opening and Nick Nick had unlocked the doors about five minutes earlier.

* * *

Coco took a look around and noticed the staff at the tail end of their preparations. The only person who looked like they weren't busy was the girl at the bar.

Coco approached the bar and said, "Excuse me."

Jena didn't respond.

"I'm sorry to bother you, but do you know where I can find Jelani?"

The girl turned her head in response to the name *Jelani* and looked at Coco. It was like she heard it, but still didn't hear it. Coco didn't need her training as a therapist to see that Jena was going through something.

"Are you OK, sweetie?" Coco asked.

Jena cracked a shy smile and looked down at the bar. She picked up a rag and began to wipe the bar counter in tight tiny circles. "I'm sorry. Just got caught up in my thoughts." She stopped wiping to look back at Coco again. "What can I do for you? You look like a dirty martini kind-a-girl."

At that moment, Coco's heart went out to Jena. She read confusion, pain, and distress on Jena's face. But instead of pressing the point, she decided to move forward with what she had come to do.

"Jelani," she said. "I'm looking for Jelani."

Jena gave a puzzled look and followed that with, "Who?"

"His car is parked right out front."

"Oh!" Jena exclaimed. "You're looking for Anthony."

Coco let out an exhaustive sigh and rolled her eyes to herself. "Yeah. Anthony."

It was now Jena's turn to sense concern in Coco's voice and body language.

"Wait a minute. Are you Anthony's little girlfriend?"

Condescension dripped from the question and Coco didn't like it at all. "I'm sorry. Who are you again?"

"Hmm," she taunted. "Well, maybe that's a question you should ask Anthony."

The line in the sand had been drawn. The two girls had just met and already didn't like each other.

But before either woman could say another word, a violent clash of bodies came tussling through the front door. One of the immaculately presented tables was knocked over as Johnnie brushed against it on his way to the floor.

"I fucking had him!"

Nick Nick stepped out of the office at the sound of the commotion. He noticed the girls at the bar and Johnnie picking himself up off of the floor.

Before Johnnie could regain his balance, Smitty manhandled him again and started dragging him across the restaurant.

Chapter 44

I followed Johnnie in but stopped at the sight of Coco. The startled look on her face matched the look of surprise on mine. Coco was focused on Johnnie being dragged through the restaurant and didn't see me walk in less than a minute after.

Coco turned around and finally saw me.

"Hey hunni!" Jena said. "You have company."

Coco looked back at Jena and cut her eyes. After giving her the look of death, she calmly walked up to me. "Is there somewhere we can talk?"

I led Coco to the opposite side of the restaurant, near Marco's office, and we sat at a table set for two. "What are you doing here?" I asked.

"I just wanted to talk. I didn't like the way our last conversation went."

"And that's it?" I asked. "You didn't have to come here for that. *Why are you here*?" I emphasized.

She had a big problem with my affiliation with Marco, so I was sure there was more to the story.

"You don't believe me?"

I didn't want to lie, so I kept my mouth closed and waited for her to answer my initial question.

"You know what, Jelani, you don't have to. That's on you. I saw your car out front and thought that there was no time better than the present to put our disagreements beyond us. That's why I'm here. I was giving you the benefit of the doubt. But after what I've seen tonight, I'm good."

Coco stood to leave and I stood up with her.

"No. You stay here," she said. "I'll make my way out."

Coco took three steps before Jena noticed her moving toward the door. Jena sang out, "Good night!"

Maybe she didn't see the tension between Coco and me, or maybe she didn't care. Maybe she wanted to cause problems.

That stopped Coco in her tracks. She turned around and walked back to me. Looking me in my eyes, she asked, "And what's up with you and her?"

Not knowing what was said between the two of them, I needed to be careful. Had Jena volunteered information? Did Coco already know?

One thing was for sure, I wasn't going to be the one to admit we had sex. There I was, caring enough to be elusive.

Maybe sleeping with Jena was a mistake. The truth was that I found myself falling for Coco. And the thought that I had done something to push her away, sobered me up quickly.

"Jelani?" Coco said. It snapped me out of my own thoughts. "Is there something I should know?"

"No. No, not at all," I found myself lying. "There's nothing between her and I."

"Anthony!" Nick Nick had yelled from Marco's office.

"Look. I have to go. I'm sorry for how I acted," I said in my most apologetic tone. "I know you care about me. I just need a better way of accepting it and showing you that I care too."

I pulled Coco in for a hug. To have her in my arms again helped me understand how much I wanted her on a more consistent basis.

"I have work to do," I continued. "Go home and I'll come through when I'm done here. We'll talk then."

Coco nodded and hugged me again and kissed me on my cheek. "Ok," she said. "Don't let them work you to death."

I walked her past Jena, to the front door. I watched as she made her way down the block. When I turned around, Nick Nick was standing at the bar, next to Jena. They were both watching me.

"Are you done?" Nick Nick asked.

He already began walking back to the office.

I followed him and when I passed by Jena, she reach a hand out and grabbed me on my arm. "You know, Anthony...I think I need to sleep at my own place tonight."

"Ok. Cool."

"What time will you be there?"

"Uh, not tonight. I think I'll be busy."

"But don't I need protection? Like last night? What do you think Nick Nick would say if he knew you was slacking on your job?"

I knew exactly what Jena was doing. She saw the connection between Coco and I. This was shocking to me. I hadn't taken Jena for the possessive or jealous type, especially since she said she was a "big girl."

"Don't worry. I'll make sure you're protected," I said. "I don't think Smitty has any plans for the night."

As much as I enjoyed the night before with Jena, I was now given a chance to build something with Coco. And that's a chance I was willing to take.

Chapter 45

When I walked into the office, Johnnie was red-faced and his eyes were swollen beyond their sockets. Watching him jumping up and down in Smitty's face reminded me of a rabid cocker spaniel barking in the face a pit bull. It was an exercise in futility. If Smitty wanted to end the madness, he could at any time. But he let Johnnie go on with his temper tantrum.

Johnnie knocked over chairs. He grabbed a glass from a crystal cocktail set and shattered it against the wall. He threw everything off the desk. He broke whatever he could get his hands on. He was in full tantrum mode.

Usually Marco would let Johnnie go through the motions, tire himself out, and then attempt to reason with him. But Nick Nick had a different approach.

Nick Nick walked between Smitty and the Tasmanian Devil. And without saying a word, he poured one glass of bourbon. It was neat. Coming back between the men, he placed the glass in front of Johnnie on Marco's bare desktop.

After putting the drink down, Nick Nick faced Johnnie, who was still making a scene. And without warning, Nick Nick slapped the hell out of Johnnie! The sound of the hit echoed and bounced between the walls. Johnnie was stunned. And then he began again.

"What the hell?! My father would never…"

Nick Nick slapped him a second time! And then again! And again! After the final hit, Johnnie fell back into the only seat that was standing. Nick Nick motioned for Smitty to set another chair upright, and he did. And Nick Nick sat beside Johnnie.

The boy sulked. Nick Nick grabbed the bourbon and shoved it into Johnnie's chest. Alcohol splashed all over the place. "Drink," Nick Nick commanded.

"Here's my problem with what you were about to do... All those fucks are calm because Marco's murder was expected. It was anticipated. A bullet in Marty's head, however, would only send people into crisis mode. His death would've been unexpected. Do you see where I'm going with this? It screws up the plan! We have the element of surprise on our side. And we need to catch them with their guard down." He turned to me.

"Anthony. Is everything set?"

"Yeah. We're good to go."

"See," Nick Nick said to Johnnie. "We're good to go. We won't jump the gun. As much as you'd like it to, this doesn't end tonight. Tomorrow will be the night those fucks pay for what they've done. Every last one of them."

* * *

I couldn't get out of the restaurant quick enough. Coco was waiting on me and she's where I needed to be. But while walking toward the door, I heard Nick Nick call out my name.

"Anthony!" He jogged to meet me at the restaurant's front door and then asked, "Where are you going?"

"Everything is settled, I'm not needed for the rest of the night."

"I hear you," Nick Nick said. "But we still have to make sure Jena is good."

"I've already got that covered Nick. Smitty will take her home and stay outside, on guard, until I get there."

"And what time will that be?"

This was a very rare passive-aggressive move on his part.

"It'll only take me a few hours Nick."

Nick Nick looked at me as if I hadn't even answered his question.

"It'll be ok." I tried to reassure him.

Nick Nick drew a deep breath. "Are you going to see that girl?" I tried to respond, but he cut me off. "Anthony, we have a good plan. But there's a chance, no matter how slight, that this may not work. And if it doesn't work, do you know what that means? All out war.

"Now if you really like her, this isn't the time to start something new. She becomes fair game. And do you want to lose her like you lost Humpty? For now, you need to be as far away from her as possible."

Even though it tore me up inside, he was right. There was no way she'd be safe if everything blew up in our face. Coco wouldn't be safe, hanging around me.

A choice had to be made. And I was both feeling *and* fighting the urge to do something I rarely do. Choose with my heart.

Chapter 46

Coco had been home long enough to change clothes, tidy up her apartment and cook a small meal. She had a taste for stir-fry and thought that Jelani would like some as well.

The California blend of broccoli, cauliflower, and carrots was a tasty mix for the chicken she grilled. Two bowls of fried rice sat out on the dining room table, waiting to be topped with her vegetables and meat. She made a bowl for herself and decided to wait on Jelani before fixing his.

She'd taken an extra minute on the way home to pick up a six-pack of Corona Light and a bottle of Maker's Mark. Looking at the bottles now, she joked to herself, "About to get this fool drunk and take advantage of him."

After cracking the red wax at the top of the bottle, she poured a little out for herself. She quickly downed the small amount of the caramel colored liquid. Her face contorted and wrinkled itself. *This is some nasty shit.*

Her attire for the evening was simple. Coco had never been the lingerie and lace kind of girl. Her oversized Drexel t-shirt hung off of one shoulder. She valued comfort over constraint.

What she wore wasn't overtly sexy, but the way the cotton t-shirt narrowed along the length of her body and hugged her small waist foretold of a coming explosion of hips and thick thighs. Sensuality oozed from her unassuming apparel. And what was most important, she knew what she was doing. Her one and only goal was seduction.

On this night, she and Jelani would stop their game of cat and mouse. She had prepared herself to be caught. And the anticipation of his visit had her elated.

Coco placed the empty glass down on the dining room table, picked up a bottle of Corona Light, and made her way to the sofa. She stretched herself out. She glanced over at the digital clock on the wall. The restaurant had been closed for a little over an hour. It wouldn't be long before Jelani was knocking on her door.

The idea brought a smirk to the beauty of her face. *Come to mama.*

Chapter 47

I didn't even get a chance to knock before my phone rang. I muffled the sound and walked a few feet away. If I could avoid it, I'd rather she didn't hear me on the phone, on the other side of her door, especially since I saw that the call was from Johnnie.

"Hey, man." There was an air of concern on my part. I felt that was the best way to address him after he just got the shit slapped out of him by Nick Nick. I wasn't certain how Johnnie had taken it and I didn't want to further irritate the situation. I didn't hear an immediate response. "You there?"

After another few seconds of silence, Johnnie finally spoke up. "Yeah, man. I'm here."

I gave Johnnie the time he needed.

"Listen, man," he finally said. "I'm really sorry."

"Don't worry about it, bruh. We got you before you got to Marty Fucker. No harm, no foul."

"It's not that." It sounded like he was searching for words. "At the hospital. I said some fucked up shit. I was angry and I shouldn't have taken it out on you. I guess I was just jealous."

"You're talking crazy."

"Shut up, man," Johnnie shot back. "Hear me out. I've always known that you were the son my father really wanted. Yeah, he loves me and would do anything for me, but when it comes to the business...you're the heir-apparent. Not me. And I'm fine with that." It sounded like Johnnie was crying. "But it's ok, man...it's ok. You are my only brother and everything our father worked for belongs to all of us. Me, you, and Jena."

"Listen to me when I say this. You have never made me feel like I was anything other than family."

"Good," Johnnie said. "Because, as family, I'm looking forward to handling our business tomorrow. When our father wakes up, we need to make sure he can live out the rest of his days doing whatever he wants to do. If that means making pizza and pasta, then so be it."

"Hey. Who knows...if we do this right, he might want to get back in the game."

"Don't hold your breath," Johnnie said, sounding more upbeat. "But I'll keep my fingers crossed, just in case."

All that needed to be said, was said. Johnnie hung up the phone, and I felt good about our talk. For a moment, I forgot where I was and what I was doing. I almost turned toward the staircase to walk down and out of the building. Then I caught myself and headed back to her front door.

I knocked three times and waited for a response. It felt like forever. I prepared to knock again and then I heard, "Hold on!" being yelled from inside.

The door opened and Jena said, "Who were you on the phone with? Johnnie? Is that why you kept me waiting?"

"Don't worry about who I was talking to," I joked.

"Hmph." She planted a hand on her hip. "And who do you think talked some sense into his head before he called you?"

I gave Jena a wild-eye look. She paid me no mind. Jena turned to walk back into her apartment.

"Don't worry!" she said. "He doesn't know! He was just making his rounds. Calling people and having a heart to heart. He was actually scared to call you, at first, and just wanted to bounce off of me what he was going to say to you. And that's it. I don't know what happened back in that office, but ever since then, he's been a different man. Granted, it's only been a few hours, but different still."

"Johnnie would bug out if he knew I was over here."

"I know." Jena waved her finger between me and her. "So let's just keep this to ourselves. No need to get him flustered. Besides, he's not the only one that would have an issue."

"Yeah. I know. Marco probably wouldn't be happy either."

"Oh. You think I'm talking about my father? Ok. So I guess Coco wouldn't give a damn then. Well, that's good to know."

At the sound of Coco's name, I instantly knew I made the wrong choice. I should have defied Nick Nick and went to her place first. But I was also confronted with the reality that I was completely drawn to Jena. I knew I shouldn't have been there, but I used what Nick Nick told me as a reason to go to her. And I used the idea that she needed protection as my reason to stay.

In all honesty, the strong feelings I had for Coco couldn't keep me away from the truth. I *wanted* to be at Jena's place. I had to recognize I was falling for both women.

Jena pulled me into her personal space by my collar, and gave me a long, passionate kiss. She broke from my lips and move instinctively to my neck, then back to my mouth.

"Yeah," she said. "It's really good to know that Coco wouldn't give a damn." She was pushing buttons for fun.

And with a half puzzled, half dumb look on my face, I let her pull me all the way in and close the door.

Chapter 48

House number six. It always had me in awe. Compared to the other houses, it was the top shelf version. Throughout the house, cinnamon colored, crushed velvet drapes hung from the ceiling and swept the floor. There was an excellent balance of polished hardwood floor and crimson Saxony carpeting.

The private rooms, with table games, were bolstered by carpeting while other communal areas, hallways and dining rooms had a hardwood accompaniment.

But by far my favorite amenity was the redbrick fireplace in the main parlor. I loved it the most because I've always had an affinity for open fires. And since House number six was the only house with a fireplace, it was easily my favorite. Nothing burned in it at the moment, but on those bitterly cold nights, it was where I'd park myself.

While I was completely in love with the interior of the house, the exterior was a different story. The brick was dingy. Black iron bars were worn outside of the doors and windows like metal braces on crooked teeth. They were for protection. No one could break in and no one could slip out.

Johnnie and I sat on bistro chairs, just a few feet away from the fireplace. The dealer had allowed us to take up his time while everyone else was rushing around, setting up for the night.

Marina's girls had been in the house for about an hour, waiting for the big spenders to arrive. Johnnie even took a couple minutes to caress a few backsides during that time. The waitstaff ran between the kitchen and the dining rooms to ensure the proper plating was in place and also to see that the cold and warm hors d'oeuvres were prepped for the opening.

"Shit!" I said. "You win again."

"Maybe we should start playing for money." Johnnie grinned.

Nick Nick walked into the parlor and joined us at the poker table. He patted the dealer on the shoulder. "Go ahead and take a break, Billy. I got this. And close the door, would you?" He watched as Billy left the room and closed the door.

"Are we clear on what happens tonight?" He stared at Johnnie. And Johnnie stared back.

"Tonight, we pick off the bosses. One by one." Johnnie wanted to show that he could be a team player. He wanted to make amends for the poor judgment of the other night.

"You're responsible for snatching Mother Mary," I said to Nick Nick. "I grab Carlito."

"And I snatch Tommy," Johnnie said.

"Good!" Nick Nick said. "And the two of you can have the pleasure of grabbing Oronzio. None of them are strangers to number six and they each have their favorite places to be. Everyone knows Marco's fondness for punctuality, so I suspect that all parties will be in the house by midnight. Give them fifteen to thirty minutes to get comfortable, and then we go get them. They'll be so much going on that no one will notice their absence.

"Mary will be monitoring the hookers on the third floor. Carlito will be shooting craps on the second. Tommy will hover around the dining room, with his greedy ass."

"And Oronzio?" I asked

"Oroznio," Nick Nick said, "will be sitting right where you are. The man loves his Texas Hold 'Em. And he, by far, will be the most difficult to snatch. The first floor is where most the action will be. Plus, I suspect that Marty Fucker will be by his side, or not too far away."

"So one of us needs to take out Fucker?" I asked.

"No. I'll cause a distraction that'll get Fucker's attention. And when I do, you two move in. Get Oronzio away from this table and then do what you have to."

Johnnie and I nodded.

"I ordered two extra commercial freezers and stashed them in the back of the kitchen. One would have been able to do the trick, but you never know. Store the bodies in the freezer. We'll leave them there until the night's end. We'll dispose of them later.

"There are only five major players in the District. After tonight, four of them will be dead. Marco can retire comfortably if he wants. Or if he decides, take over the whole damn city. This is a great plan, Anthony. Now let's get to work, fellas."

Johnnie and I pushed away from the poker table to make our way out of the parlor. Before leaving the room, Johnnie looked back and asked, "The distraction for Marty Fucker? What will it be?"

"Don't worry," Nick Nick said. "When it happens, you'll know."

Chapter 49

From a second story window, we could look past the bars and see a steady stream of guests filing into the house. Mother Mary, Carlito, and Tommy had already made their way in. There were also a host of lower level players who came out because they heard that this was the curtain call for Ribisi's gambling houses.

"Have you seen Oronzio yet?" Johnnie asked. "Are we sure he's coming?"

"Calm down. He'll be here. Might be running behind. Just chill."

"I want Oronzio! Everyone else is just a side dish. He's the main meal. If he doesn't show, we'll have to go after him, you know that, right?"

I started to tune Johnnie out. He was going on autopilot, ready to react without thinking it through. I understood his frustration, but I chose not to play into it. And then I saw them.

"Look!" I said. "Up the street." I pointed in the direction of Oronzio and Marty Fucker. They were slowly walking toward the house.

"Why are they walking so slow? You think they know what's up?"

"Johnnie…"

"Calm down, I know," he said before I could get it out. That was a good sign. Self-correction meant that he was learning. And then I saw something that did have me worried. Or perplexed may have been a better way to describe it.

Marty Fucker and Oronzio were arguing. It was hard to tell what the problem was, but it was clear that it was more than a minor disagreement. What happened next changed everything for us.

"Where the fuck is he going?!"

Marty Fucker snatched his arm away from Oronzio. There were a few more words and Marty turned around to leave. He was going back in the direction that they came from. "Do you think he's headed to the car?" But it was clear he was going back to the car.

"This is good, isn't it?" Johnnie asked. "Without Marty, won't it be easier to get Oronzio?" His question hung in the air. "But you know what, if Marty's not here in this house, then we can't know for certain where he is. Can we? We run the risk of him ruining everything! Fuck! We need him in the house."

"Exactly."

"Well, it's not midnight yet. We've got 15 minutes. That's enough time to go get him," Johnnie said.

"Knock him out?" I turned from the window.

"Drag him back."

"Nick Nick said we had two freezers, just in case."

"I think this qualifies as a 'just in case' scenario," Johnnie said. "If we head out the back door and down the alley, we might be able to head him off before he gets to his car and leaves. Together, we can take him and be back before twelve."

I gave it thought for a split second, but my mind was already made up. Johnnie was right. We peeked out of the room and down the hall to make sure Nick Nick wasn't around. We heard his voice coming from the front of the house, which was away from where we wanted to go, so we were in the clear.

Down the stairs we went. Out the kitchen door, leading to the back alley. Running as fast as we could.

Chapter 50

"I don't like it!" Marty Fucker objected. "Fuck him! He can keep his comp chips!"

"Do we have to go through this again?" Oronzio said. He stopped walking to give Marty a minute to vent.

"Come on man! You know what this is about."

"You're absolutely right!" Oronzio shot back. "But do *you* know what this is about? It's about these gambling houses finally being up for grabs. It's about adding another piece to our enterprise. It's about playing nice until you get what you want. Then, and only then, can you burn someone else's house down. But first, you have to solidify your own standing.

"You think Mary, Tommy or Carlito have the structure or manpower to operate houses throughout the city? No! So let's play nice, smile in these people's faces, and then make sure that Marco is completely out of the way before making moves of our own. Do you understand?"

Marty wasn't feeling Oronzio's train of thought. He snatched his arm away.

"Maybe you should go back to the car and give some thought to this. Come back once you've calmed the fuck down."

Turning to walk away, Marty looked back. "How can you do business with that man? He's not even a man. He's a fucking snake."

As Marty walked back to the car, Oronzio called out to him. "Marty! It's just temporary! He's as good as dead! And in this business, we're all snakes!"

Chapter 51

We were slightly winded by the time we reached the end of the alley. We stayed against the wall where the shadows made it easy to find cover in the darkness that surrounded us. I popped my head out and looked quickly around the corner. Marty Fucker was on his way.

I could hear him cursing out loud. An angry fire. It seeped from his body. That's probably why he didn't notice me. I looked straight ahead to see that his car was in front of us.

Surveying the ground of the alley, I found a long rectangular sheet of metal that looked a lot like a slim jim. It was lying on the ground next to Johnnie's foot.

I picked it up. "Ok. Just like we said. Hopefully, this makes it more believable."

Johnnie nodded and I slipped out onto the sidewalk. I approached Marty's car with my back toward him so he couldn't see my face. I jammed the make shift slim jim between the car frame and the window.

My goal wasn't to steal the car. It was to get Marty's attention. And it worked. It only took ten seconds before Marty was behind me. The steel of his gun was pressed against the back of my head.

"What the fuck do you think you're doing? This is definitely not your lucky night," Marty said.

I dropped the slim jim like it was a hot potato and raised my hands above my head. I wanted him to see that I was unarmed. Turning slowly to face Marty, I could see the look of surprise register over his face.

"Anthony!"

And before he could say another word, Johnnie jumped Marty from behind. The element of surprise worked perfectly. Johnnie slapped Marty twice on the back of his head with the butt of a gun and he went down.

"Damn. Did you kill him?" I asked.

Johnnie shoved Marty's limp body with his foot. "Nah, he ain't dead. Not yet."

Chapter 52

Three dark figures, dressed in black and ski masks, stood in the alley behind House number six. Two of them grabbed a steel extension ladder that happened to be conveniently left on the ground three houses away.

They propped the ladder against the house as one of the dark figures pulled its rope to slide the top half of the ladder to the roof with ease. The music and loud indecipherable conversations vibrating through the brick of the house overpowered the clanking and clunking from the ladder.

One man held the ladder in place and kept a constant survey of the alley. Another climbed the ladder. The third took a padlock and heavy-duty zinc-plated tow chain out of a black knapsack. The chains jingled as he scurried around to the front of the house.

Once on the roof, the masked man pulled the sleeve of his black turtleneck sweater back to expose a digital watch. The timepiece read 11:59. He walked to the front of the house and peered over the edge to see his partner weaving the chain through the frame of the black iron gate and securing it with the lock. After giving a couple of tugs to ensure that no one would be able to get in or out, he extended a "thumbs up" toward the roof.

The masked man looked at his watch again and this time it read 12:00. It was midnight. It was time. He turned to his right and found the five-gallon containers. There were three of them sitting next to chimney. The containers had been left there for him, earlier in the day just like the ladder was in the alley.

He grabbed the first of them, lifted it to the opening in the chimney and poured the liquid. He poured until the container was empty.

Then he reached for the second one.

* * *

The clear liquid advanced out of the fireplace like a tiny army, invading foreign land. The gambling patrons didn't notice a thing. It only had a few inches to go before it found its way to the Saxony carpet in the main parlor. And that's how it was able to spread throughout the room. It soaked its way through.

Drunk off of alcohol, sex, and the excitement of huge cash payouts, everyone obliviously partied along. The scent of gasoline was veiled by the night's debauchery. By the time the kitchen staff detected the smell, it was too late. The entire main parlor seeped with the flammable liquid.

The patrons were still clueless, but the kitchen staff inspected each of the industrial stoves for gas leaks. The odor had gotten stronger. They found nothing. The ovens were intact and functioning properly. The only thing of interest was a skinny stream of liquid that found its way into a puddle, a few feet beyond the kitchen portal.

It caught the attention of one of the kitchen staff, so he followed the stream through the house. It led back to the main parlor. He looked in and couldn't believe how no one noticed the overwhelming smell. Upon stepping in the room, his shoe sank into the wet carpet. When he lifted his foot, a soaking wet, semi-permanent imprint of a size eleven shoe was left in its place.

That's when the horror of the situation sank in. The parlor was saturated in gasoline.

* * *

After emptying all three of the containers, the masked man walked between the front and back of the house. He monitored the actions of the men below. Each was responsible for chaining and padlocking the iron gates on the doors and then dowsing the structure with gasoline.

The men moved quickly. The longer they took, the greater risk of being caught or seen. So speed was essential.

Windows, doors, and the brick wall itself...everything dripped. After being sufficiently pleased with what he saw, the man on the roof pulled a red road flare from his back pocket. He took a second to remove the cap and then rub the striking surface against the button. And then there was fire.

The masked man walked past the chimney on his way back to the ladder. As he passed it, he casually dropped the red stick into the gas-soaked chimney shaft. The roar of a fireball whirled as the flare traveled downward. Simultaneously, flames shot upward.

And then...there was fire.

The man on the roof slid down the ladder and reached the ground right before his partners set fire to the outside of House number six. They reunited and hurried to the end of the alley where a black SUV waited for them.

Jumping in the back seat of the truck, navy blue suit guy and Baldie sat up front, watching as a reddish glow emanated from the alley. Satisfied with the quickness and efficiency of the job, the two men smiled, and the truck sped away.

Chapter 53

"Maybe we didn't think this one all the way through," Johnnie said, while we stood over Marty.

"Fuck. You might be right. How the hell are we going to get him in the house without being noticed? If someone sees us dragging a passed out man back to the house..."

"And not just any passed out man," Johnnie said.

"Right. And we can't just stand here."

Johnnie glanced at the trunk of Marty's car. "We can always come back for him later."

Knowing that as long as we stood on the sidewalk with Marty passed out between us, our odds of being seen by someone increased by the second. Johnnie didn't hesitate to rummage through Marty's pockets. "Got it!" He threw me the keys and I immediately opened the trunk.

Inside I saw the regular things you'd find in a car trunk. Spare tire, tire iron, canister of gas, and a few road flares. But I also found a long line of sturdy rope.

First I tossed anything that could be used by Marty out of the trunk and onto the ground. The road flares, gasoline, and tire iron had to go. I figured it was safe to leave everything else in place.

When I emerged from the trunk with rope in hand, Johnnie had ripped a large chuck of Marty's shirt off of him. "Here." He threw it to me. "We can use this to gag him.

And while I was going through the trunk, I could see that Johnnie went on a little scavenger hunt too. He removed Marty's back holster that held his axe. It also had a little side holster, which held a smaller hatchet, attached to it.

I scooped up Marty and body slammed him into the trunk. I carefully gagged and tied him up. I wanted to make sure he was bound in a manner that would ensure his presence on our return. Johnnie had taken a minute to toss all the discarded items, including the axe and hatchet, in the back seat of the car.

"This should do for now. We need to make it back. It's already a couple minutes past twelve," I said.

We were already headed back down the alley. "You think Nick Nick is looking for us?"

"I don't think we're that late," I said, looking in Johnnie's direction, who was by my side. But only briefly.

Johnnie stopped in his tracks. Weird lights reflected in his horror-filled eyes.

I stopped. "What's wrong now?!"

"That!" was his only response. He pointed into the alley in the direction we were headed. And I didn't see it at first. I was so pumped up from getting the drop on the Hatchet, and worried about Nick Nick looking for us, that I completely missed the reddish-orange glow coming from the middle of the alley.

It finally hit me; the smell of gasoline, charred wood, and burning flesh. Embers danced between the houses and the brick wall across from them. Something was on fire and Johnnie knew exactly what that something was. House number six.

"Not again!" Johnnie shouted. And without warning, he bolted past me.

Johnnie reached the house before I did. Well, as close as he could get. The deeper we ran into the alley, the hotter it was. By the time we got there, flames raged from out of the windows.

I could see through the flickering of the blaze that there were chains on the door. I also noticed a couple of gas containers sprawled on the ground. And that was all I needed to see.

"Johnnie." I said. "It's time to go. We can't do anything else here." Fire engines could be heard off in the distance. I tugged on Johnnie's arm so we could head back the way we came. He snatched it from me. "We've got to go!"

Johnnie faced me and I could see him beginning to tear up. I didn't know what to make of it until he spoke. "Did we actually see Oronzio walk into the house?" It was Johnnie's anger over how Oronzio was playing us that moved him to tears.

The sirens were racing closer.

"Did we actually *SEE* him?!" He yelled.

"No. We didn't."

"We need to know where the hell he is. And only one person can tell us. Marty."

"Well, let's go then. And I have the perfect place to take him."

We ran away from the last of the gambling houses. By this time, it was being broken down by fire. We ran in the direction we had previously come. Away from the sirens and back toward the Hatchet.

Chapter 54

Navy blue suit guy and Baldie walked into the living room of the row house that served as their headquarters. All the major players were supposed to meet back there after the fire was started.

There was already someone waiting for them. Marina stood near the window and felt the heat from the burning house. The headquarters sat boldly across the street. It was the perfect place to monitor the operation.

Marina turned around as soon as she heard the men walk in. She was holding herself with one arm wrapped around her body. The other was perpendicular, with her hand in her mouth. She was biting her nails. She moved her hand from her face long enough to ask, "Where is he?"

"On his way," Baldie said.

"He was right behind us," navy blue suit guy said, taking a seat.

Barely satisfied with their response, Marina decided to ask them about the job. "Did it go smoothly? Did anyone see you?"

"The house is on fire, isn't it?" the bald one said.

"What about the hospital?" she prodded. "You're still going, right?"

After having orchestrated what would probably go down as the city's most notorious arson, the men were exhausted and seriously annoyed by the questions.

"No." Navy blue suit guy said with the roll of his eyes. "We're not."

"What a minute!" Marina shot back. "No no no! That's not good. You have to go to hospital. This isn't over until Marco Ribisi is dead."

The two men looked at each other. Baldie took a sigh and told her something that she wasn't aware of. "There's been a change of plans."

"What change of plans?!"

Just then, the sound of a closing door caught everyone's attention. They turned to see the mastermind of the night's activities walk across the living room. He grabbed Marina by her waist and pulled her in for a long and passionate kiss.

Once he was done, he said, "Gentlemen, that's how you shut a beautiful woman's mouth."

She smiled for the first time and said, "That's what you think. Now what about these new plans? Care to share it with me, Nick?"

* * *

Nick Nick and Marina met decades ago, when Nick Nick was an independent contract killer. Long before he found himself in allegiance to anyone in the DC area, Nick Nick was the best hit man that money could buy. And he happened to come across Marina as a result of negotiating a contract with a new client, Marina's husband, Dmitry.

There was a competitor in Richmond, VA, that was encroaching upon the DC market. Over the matter of months, Dmitry noticed that there was less demand for his girls. He would have bet his last dollar that his clients hadn't caught religion and grew a conscious all of a sudden. So for Dmitry this was an obvious sign that supply had risen and new girls were coming in from elsewhere.

When Nick Nick arrived at their home, Marina had answered the door. At the moment he first saw her, the chemistry was so strong that he knew working anywhere near her would present a problem. As soon as he laid eyes on her, it was like he was hit with a lightning bolt. Electricity coursed through him. Love at first sight was something Nick Nick wasn't prone to believing in. But he was light-headed around her and couldn't deny what he was feeling.

Marina was attracted to him as well. What made it worse, she and Dmitry would go through months without making love and they happened to be in their dry spell when she met Nick Nick. So when she saw him, she could have ripped him apart right then. But she maintained her composure. Marina escorted Nick Nick to Dmitry's office where they discussed the terms of the contract. After that, Nick Nick left to conduct the agreed upon business.

It would be weeks before he returned to Dmitry and Marina's home. He had been looking for Dmitry to "discuss more business," or at least that's what he told Marina. But he already knew that Dmitry was nowhere around and Marina would be home alone. He had been thinking about her, night and day, since they met. This was his chance to get her all to himself. So he took advantage of the moment.

Nick Nick relied heavily on intuition. He wasn't a reckless man. But there was something in how Marina looked at him when they first locked eyes.

He saw pain. Marina was sick with neglect. He knew there was a void, an emotional black hole. Emptiness. In their brief interaction, Nick Nick saw himself as the cure for all that kept her ill. He had come back to make her whole again.

"Is Dmitry in?" Nick Nick said, while standing at the front door.

Marina took him in with her eyes. "You didn't come here for Dmitry, did you?"

Attracted to her forward nature, he said, "Maybe I have. Maybe I haven't."

"Well, that's a shame. So unsure."

"If that's the case, then I'm busted. Maybe you should invite me in and teach me how to be more decisive."

And Marina did just that. She invited him in. Their love affair had begun. And it lasted years. Marina was no longer concerned with the lack of affection from her husband. Nick Nick had cured her. She was in love again.

This sudden change in her personality was ultimately noticed by her husband, but by then, they were a year into their affair. Dmitry assumed that she was seeing someone else, but he had no idea who the person was. The idea of her infidelity was unbearable. He never thought that Marina was capable of such a thing. He had no confirmation, so he kept his suspicions to himself. He chose not to confront his wife.

Being the possessive and controlling person that he was, he knew exactly what would bring her back into the fold. He convinced Marina that he wanted a child. Marina had wanted a baby for years, and to finally hear that Dmitry was ready made her ecstatic.

She told Nick Nick of the new development and made him promise to leave her alone. Even though it was a decision that would hurt her as well, she needed his buy-in in order to remain committed to her husband and the new family they were about to begin.

Nick Nick was heartbroken, but agreed. Dmitry and Marina began trying to conceive. Six weeks later, she was pregnant.

It was years before they saw each other again. During that time, Dmitry died. The child they had together had become a young man. Nick Nick had gained the trust of Marco Ribisi and became his most trusted advisor. But the years away from Marina made him a bitter man. The lost love made him a hateful one too. He had never found another woman like Marina.

She had taken over her husband's business and also become the point person for all illegal activities in DC. It was at Nick Nick's first meeting with the bosses that they saw each other. And he fell in love, all over again.

They rekindled their relationship but decided to keep it to themselves. They spent years making love in the shadows. They spent years, plotting and planning. They spent years, methodically moving toward the day that they would own the District of Columbia.

And that day had finally come.

* * *

"Yes, hun. The plans have changed. The boys weren't in the house when the fire was started. I've got to deal with them before I can deal with anything else," Nick Nick said.

"And how do you plan to do that?" Marina asked.

"We're going to the restaurant. And then...I'm going to make them come to me."

Chapter 55

The headlights from Marty Fucker's car shone brightly into the deserted tunnel. I was leaning against a wall and Johnnie was manhandling the Hatchet. He dragged the groggy and limp man to the middle of the tunnel with one hand and carried a canister of gasoline with the other. One of the emergency flares stuck out of his back pocket.

"Yeah, this is it," Johnnie said. He tossed the Hatchet to the ground and set the canister down a few feet away. Marty lay there for a moment and then attempted to sit up on his knees. He swayed from side to side.

"You're making a big mistake," Marty said with a slur.

Johnnie hit him across the jaw with force. Knocking him back to the ground. "Shut up!" He grabbed the gasoline and started pouring it on the Hatchet. It splashed everywhere.

"Wait! Stop!" Marty yelled. "Don't do this!"

Johnnie continued to dump the gasoline over him until the container was nearly empty.

"You can go to hell," Johnnie said. He grabbed the flare from his back pocket.

"Hold on," I said before he ignited the red stick. "Marty. Do you know where you are right now? Where it's all coming to an end?"

His gasoline dripped head slowly turned toward me. There was an air of defeat to each inch of his movement. He looked around and squinted his eyes, taking in as much of the tunnel he could see.

There were large letters, spray-painted in red, directly behind me. He put them together and read the words aloud. "I WILL KILL YOU ALL." He looked down and chuckled to himself. His chuckle grew into a hysterical laugh.

"What's so fuckin' funny?" Johnnie asked.

"The brilliant irony. Ask Anthony."

"Bunnyman Bridge," I said.

"Virginia," Marty responded.

"The urban legend says there's a man in a bunny suit running around these parts killing people. He's been doing it for years, since the Seventies, the legend says."

"Uh...I just wanna kill this fuck! Who cares about some man playing Halloween year round?"

"Bunnyman has a weapon of choice," I explained.

The Hatchet turned toward his car and could see his axe and hatchet piled together on the ground. "Weapon of choice were always hatchets, Johnnie. It's a well-known tale in Washington. And now I'm going to die in the place where the legend of the hatchet wielding Bunnyman came to be."

"Yes, you are. But before you die, you've got to tell us where we can find Oronzio. Give us what we need, and instead of barbecuing you, maybe we'll just shoot you in the head. Get it over quick."

"Find Oronzio?" Marty gasped. "You've had me locked in a trunk, I'm soaked in gas, and you're asking me where to find Oronzio?! Fuck! I don't know! He should be right where you left him. Having a ball at the house, I suppose!"

When he said, "...at the house," Johnnie and I looked at each other.

Our confusion was evident. So I asked the question that lingered between the two of us. "What do you mean by, 'at the house?'"

Chapter 56

Jena pulled the chair closer to her father's hospital bed. Marco was tied into so many tubes. They were coming out of everywhere. None were as scary to Jena as the huge one protruding from Marco's mouth.

Jena grabbed Marco's hand that was closest to her. "Dr. Adenuga said that we should talk to you as much as possible. He said that sometimes coma patients hear the voices of loved ones and respond by squeezing their hand.

"Can you hear me?" she asked. "If you can, squeeze my hand dad." Jena waited for a few moments, hoping to get a response. But none came. Instead tears began to roll down Jena's face like molasses.

"I have something to tell you. It's about House number six. It's gone, dad. I know you were closing it anyway. But I heard on the news that there was a fire. Chains were found on the doors and everyone was locked inside. It's a graveyard now."

Jena's tears began to roll heavier and faster. "And I can't get in touch with Nick Nick or the boys. Nobody knows where they are. I'm scared. You might be all I have left.

"Don't leave me dad. Please."

Jena began crying uncontrollably. She was slumped over her father's non-responsive body. This was the first time she had let her emotions go. Her strength crumbled under the prospect of living the rest of her life without the only men she ever loved. Johnnie. Anthony. Nick Nick. Her father.

Even through the echo of her sobbing, Jena heard a tentative tap at the door. She looked up and tried to fix herself as best as possible.

"Come in," she said.

Smitty cracked the door. "Hey princess. I have some good news. Nick Nick's been in touch with me."

The news certainly was good and perked her right up. She stood and took a couple steps toward the door. "And the fellas?"

"I've got to get you to the restaurant. Nick Nick says that Johnnie and Anthony will meet us there."

"Wait, no! I'm not leaving my father! There were chains on the doors at the house. Dad isn't safe!"

"Nick Nick has your father covered." The massive man moved to the side. Detective Daniels was standing behind him. Jena relaxed a little at the sight of the badge clipped to his belt. "You'll take care of him?"

"Don't worry. Get out of here." Detective Daniels said with a smile. "I'll be here all night."

That was enough for Jena. She rush back to Marco, grabbed his hand again and kissed him on his forehead. "Everything's going to be ok, dad. I'm about to meet Nick Nick back at the restaurant. I'll stop through and see you tomorrow. I love you."

And just as she was about to release him, she felt the most unexpected and amazing thing. Marco squeezed her hand.

Chapter 57

Nick Nick sat in the back seat of the black SUV. Baldie was behind the wheel and the man in the navy blue suit sat beside him.

They pulled over, in front of an apartment building. "Is this it?" Nick Nick asked.

"Mmm hmm," Baldie said.

The navy blue suit guy had his head out the window and was looking up the street. "Wait a minute. Isn't that her?"

There was a woman jogging at a steady rhythmic pace toward the spot they had parked. It was Coco, wrapping up one of her routine late night runs.

Nick Nick recognized her immediately. He was the only one to exit the truck. It took Coco a little longer to recognize him, but once she did, her pace slowed down to a walk, just about fifteen feet before reaching him.

Nick Nick didn't wait for Coco to address him. "Coco, my dear, I need to have a word with you."

Coco stared at Nick Nick, not knowing what to make of this man, whom she barely knew, showing up on her doorstep.

"Is Jelani ok?"

"Oh Christ! I'm sorry," Nick Nick said, trying to appear considerate. "Let me say up front that Jelani," using his birth name purposefully, "is perfectly fine."

Coco must have been holding her breath because upon hearing that, she let out a sigh of relief.

"But he asked me to bring you to the restaurant. Some things have transpired tonight that now make it unsafe for you to be by yourself." Nick Nick took a few steps closer to Coco. "With that said, you need to come with me."

Coco immediately backed up. "I'm sorry, but I don't really know you like that. And I don't know what's going on, so..."

He interrupted her before she could finish. "Precisely. You don't know what's going on. Which means, you have no idea how much danger you're in. Things are spiraling out of control and we need to move quickly." He paused for dramatic effect. "Have you ever wondered what it was that Jelani did for us?"

"He's a restaurant host," she stuttered.

Nick Nick gazed at her intensely. "You're not that naive. What he *really* does." Nick Nick waited for a response, but none came. "I can't force you to come with me but trust me when I say, you're not safe alone."

She still didn't move.

"When Anthony...I mean Jelani," it was a slip. "asks me to do something; I've got to get it done. Or there's a price to pay. Help me help you. Get in the truck. Let's go to the restaurant. And once there, I'll answer any question you have."

Coco considered it for a few seconds. "Any question I have?"

"Whatever you wanna know."

Coco thought about the prospect of finally getting answers to the questions that had kept a wedge between her and Jelani. This was her chance to satisfy her inquisitive mind. The nosey nature of hers made a strong argument for getting in the truck.

As Coco walked to the car, the navy blue suit guy stepped out of the front passenger seat to open the back door. There was something about his rushed movements that startled her. Maybe she wasn't prepared. Maybe it was because he was yet another stranger. Or possibly it was because he didn't look to be nearly as inviting as Nick Nick.

Whatever it was, her rational mind began to speak a lot louder than her nosey nature. She looked at the man in the blue suit and no longer felt like taking a ride with them was a good idea.

Coco turned around and looked at Nick Nick. "You know what, I'm not too comfortable with this. I'll just call Jelani and tell him I decided not to come. I'm sure he'll understand it had nothing to do with you." She hurried past Nick Nick and jogged up the front steps of her apartment building.

Coco unzipped the small pouch on the back of her jogging pants and pulled out her set of keys. She fumbled through finding the right key and attempted to unlock the door. Her hands shook to the point where she couldn't control the jingling of her keys.

Before she could get the right key in the keyhole, Nick Nick had already waved his hand and the navy blue suit guy bolted up the stairs. He grabbed Coco by her waist and hoisted her into the air, carrying her back toward the truck.

It was futile but Coco kicked and screamed. There was no one around and the man was too strong. Nick Nick shook his head as they passed him.

Coco was thrown into the back seat and her abductor hopped in right after, to keep her contained. Nick Nick walked to the front passenger-side door, which was still open. Before getting in, he looked back at Coco.

"Didn't I say you was in danger?"

Chapter 58

Nick Nick walked into Marco's Restaurant with navy blue suit guy practically dragging Coco in behind him. The bald one remained at the front door.

Before they made it to Marco's office, Nick Nick caught Smitty and Jena walking up to the door, out of the corner of his eye. He rushed navy blue suit guy into the office, to keep Coco out of their line of sight.

When Smitty reached the door, Baldie, held up his hand to stop him from walking any further. "Thanks. I'll take it from here." He pulled Jena closer by her arm.

The surprise on Jena's face was evident. She didn't know what was going on. And neither did Smitty.

"What gives?" Smitty saw Nick Nick standing in the restaurant and called out to him. "Hey Nick! What's going on man?!"

"Thanks, Smitty!" Nick Nick called back out to him, with the wave of a hand. "We're good now! Have a good night!"

Jena gave Smitty a disconcerted look. And Smitty didn't know what to make of the situation. If he wanted to force his way through the door, with his size and strength, he could have. But he felt that would cause bigger problems. It was best to play along for the moment.

"Ok. You all have a good night then." And with that, Smitty retreated away from the building and headed in the direction of the street corner.

Baldie passed Jena on to Nick Nick, who walked her to the Marco's office. "Umm. What's going on, Nick? And who are these guys?"

He didn't answer.

Navy blue suit guy came out of the office to retrieve Jena. "Nick?" she said again, louder. "What's going on?" Navy blue suit guy tugged Jena into the office and slammed the door shut.

Nick Nick could hear a slight struggle beyond the closed door. "Nick!" was screamed from the other side. There were more sounds of struggle. And then silence.

The door opened and navy blue suit guy emerged from the room slightly disheveled. "Are they secured?" Nick Nick asked.

"Don't worry. They're not going anywhere."

"Good. Johnnie and Anthony will come for them. Just make sure you're ready. In the meantime, no one gets in or out. Understood?"

"Understood."

"That's what I like to hear." Nick Nick turned to leave the restaurant. He called out to both of the men as he left. "Hold down the fort, gentlemen. There's only one thing left for me to do."

"The hospital?" Baldie asked.

But by that time, Nick Nick had already disappeared.

Chapter 59

BEEP.

The monitor was slowly starting to get on Daniels' nerve. He sat in the chair next to Marco. The accompanying silence didn't bother him. But the intermittent noise was giving him all that he could take.

BEEP.

If I suffocated him right now, would the sound stop? Daniels knew that once the sun came up, a new era would also dawn in DC. Marco played no part in this new era and his death was only a matter of when, not if.

BEEP.

It felt like hours. When were these guys coming? Daniels was ready to go.

BEEP.

The door to the room cracked open. "Thank God," he muttered to himself.

Nick Nick walked in.

"I was expecting your pit bulls. Not you," Daniels said.

"They're at the restaurant." Nick Nick walked to Marco's comatose body. "A restaurant, you may never see again, my friend." He patted Marco's arm as he spoke.

"What happens now?"

"Now? Marco and I have a little heart to heart. And you..." Nick Nick pulled out his cell phone and checked the time. "You should go meet the guys back that the restaurant. They'll need your help soon."

Daniels didn't question the command. He was thrilled to leave that hospital. He gathered his things and headed out the door, leaving Marco and Nick Nick alone to have their "heart to heart," as Nick Nick put it.

Daniels took a last look into the room before walking out. Marco was lying in the bed. Nick Nick was sitting in the chair, beside him, with his cell phone still in hand. The door closed slowly behind Daniels.

The last thing he heard was... BEEP.

Chapter 60

The train passing, overhead, gave me a minute to think. We had to stop because it was too loud to talk.

Marty's "at the house" response to my question didn't make sense. For Marty to think that Oronzio was still at the house and enjoying a night of gambling meant he had no idea the house had burned to the ground. And if he had no idea, then that meant Oronzio hadn't planned the fire.

The passing train gave Marty time to think as well. "What the fuck! You bring me all the way out here to find someone I left with you? Have you lost someone, Anthony?" he said with a hint of sarcasm.

Johnnie wasn't in the mood for it. "Keep talking shit!" he said as he struck Marty across the jaw.

Marty spit out a mixture of blood, saliva, and gasoline.

"Where the fuck is Oronzio?!" Johnnie yelled at the top of his lungs and poured more fuel over Marty. Marty bounced around in a horrible effort of escaping the liquid that continued to drip all around him. "Where is he?!"

"Stop," I said to Johnnie. "Marty. Look at me." He took his attention away from Johnnie and fixed a stare on me. "The house was destroyed by fire. The doors were chained shut. Everyone inside is dead. And you mean to tell me that your boss had nothing to do with it?"

The next moment was a critical one. I knew it would tell us everything we needed to know about Oronzio's involvement with the house being burned down. What I was looking for didn't take long to surface.

The spark in Marty's eyes could have ignited the gasoline all over him. He bounced around even more. He was livid. "That fucking snake!" he yelled. "I'll kill him! Let! Me! GO!"

Marty had exerted so much energy that he made himself tired. He realized that his struggling would get him nowhere. He started to calm down a bit...at least enough for me to ask another question.

"Was Oronzio in the house?"

The horn from the train that just passed over us could be heard off in the distance. It was the only sound for the moment. Everything else stood still. Johnnie and I waited for an answer. And it looked like Marty couldn't bring himself to provide it.

"I guess he likes the taste of gasoline then..." Johnnie tipped the canister over Marty, who didn't struggle or fight against him this time. "Because I can't hear him."

Johnnie stopped for a second and looked back at me. He couldn't understand Marty's non-responsive demeanor. And that's when Marty spoke softly. "I was supposed to come back for him in an hour. He was only staying for an hour."

I stepped closer in order to hear him better. And next, all I heard was laughter. It started as a low chuckle and then became progressively louder. Marty was laughing to himself.

Once it looked like he got the giggles out of his system, he spoke and sounded defeated. "I tried to warn him. But he didn't listen." It looked like he was thinking aloud, because he certainly wasn't addressing us.

"Marty!" I yelled to snap him out of his trance.

He looked up and spoke to us again. "You all think you're so fucking smart. You had a snake in your front yard this whole time. You wanna know who burned down your party and killed all those people? Then you need to look in-house. You need to look at Dominic Nicholas."

"Nick Nick? You think we're that stupid?"

"He's lying," Johnnie shot back. He reached for the emergency flare in his back pocket. "Let me set this fool on fire."

"No. Wait." I held my hand out in front of Johnnie. "Marty. What are you talking about? How was it Nick Nick? We already know Oronzio wanted the business. We already know he had Humpty and Skinny Vinnie killed to stop us from connecting the dots. And not to mention he also tried to have me knocked off too. We know it all."

"Like I said, you all think you're so fucking smart. I'll let you in on a little secret. There was no reason to kill Humpty. He was working for us!"

Chapter 61

"He's playing us." I couldn't believe it. We stepped away to the car so we could talk without being heard. I found it hard to believe that my closest friend decided to work as a spy for Oronzio. And that's exactly what Marty was saying.

According to him, Humpty was reporting to the Oronzio organization everything he was doing while he was on the payroll for Marco.

"But what if he's telling the truth?" Johnnie said. "We're assuming that Nick Nick was in the fire. Just like we assumed Oronzio wasn't. As much as I'd like to light him up like a fourth of July firecracker, we have to hear him out."

I reluctantly agreed and we made our way back to Marty, but Johnnie took the lead. "Marty. Make me believe you. You want to get Nick Nick?"

"In the worst way."

"Ok. Then break it down."

Over the next few minutes, Marty talked about how my time away from the Ribisi family was the start of it all. During my hiatus, or sabbatical, or vacation, or whatever you want to call it, Humpty stepped in. But we knew that already.

No one knew why I had disappeared. So Humpty made assumptions along with everyone else. The misconception was that Marco and I had a falling out, and as a result, I was no longer on the inside.

Without anyone confirming or denying, Humpty became irate with the idea that the Ribisi family had cut me out. Especially considering that since Nick Nick had gotten older, the family leaned on me to do all the dirty work.

For Humpty, his allegiance was to me, not the people I worked for.

That's when he approached Oronzio to organize a huge "Fuck you!" to Marco Ribisi. His thought was that he'd volunteer to do a little work, gain as much information on the Ribisi's as possible, and then sell it to Oronzio.

In the beginning it was slow churning. Humpty hadn't come across anything that was useful. It took about four months before Humpty had hit the jackpot.

Using the surveillance package that I originally initiated, he captured video and audio that turned everything upside down. Humpty accidentally captured Nick Nick on tape talking about his plans for eliminating Marco and taking over the gambling houses.

Humpty brought the footage to Oronzio. But for Oronzio to be the sole owner of this information, he had to pay for it. Fifty thousand dollars.

Nick Nick ultimately caught on to Humpty. Whether it was luck, intuition, or just downright not trusting him, he had used his own resources to follow Humpty and discovered what he was doing.

Nick Nick found out about the video and Humpty's intention to sell it to Oronzio. So he took it upon himself to set up a fake meeting where he would have Humpty killed and secure the video. And at that point, avert a catastrophe that would've derailed his plans of taking over Marco's business.

Chapter 62

"I don't believe him," Johnnie said, turning to me.

"Neither do I. Set his ass on fire."

Johnnie hadn't even waited for me to finish my statement before he ignited the flare. Sparks jumped off of the stick. The tunnel now had a reddish glow.

"Stop! No!" Marty pleaded. "Don't do this! I'm telling the truth!"

"Shut up!" Johnnie yelled. He kicked Marty in the chest and he slid back a couple of feet. "Clearly you're not trying to help us out here. We'll find Oronzio on our own. Any last words, Fucker? And if you have something to say, please make sure it's nothing like the bullshit you just tried feeding us."

Johnnie walked closer to Marty and was ready to toss the flare, but to me, he was entirely too close. With all of the fuel splashed around, I know a good amount landed on him. I didn't want Johnnie to go up in flames with Marty. "Uh, Johnnie," I said.

"What?!" Annoyed by my interruption.

"You think you might want to take a step back?"

Johnnie looked around and immediately got the point. "Oh shit! You're right, man." He took a few steps backwards, while keeping his eyes locked on a dejected Marty.

"This is it, Marty. Time to say good night," I said.

Accepting the reality of the situation, Marty gathered himself up on his knees. His back was not bent, but straight. "Fuck you," he said. "If you're going to do it... Do it now."

And without hesitation Johnnie swung his arm back to lob the ignited flare onto the gasoline soaked Marty Fucker. But before he could release the stick, his cell phone rang.

The electronic sound of the phone rang above the hissing of the burning flare. And the sound stopped Johnnie's arm in mid-swing. He threw the flare off to the side and started patting his body in search of his phone.

"What the fuck is the problem?" I asked.

"That ring! I gave everyone a personalized ringtone." Johnnie said as he fumbled to pull his phone out of his pants pocket. "It can't be."

Johnnie seemed to already know who was calling him before looking at the caller ID. Bewildered, he looked at the screen and then extended it toward me.

After reading the flashing name, my heart sank into my stomach. Marty must have been telling the truth all along. The name on the phone read NICK NICK.

* * *

When the metallic tint of Nick Nick's voice came across Johnnie's cell phone, it sent chills down my spine.

"Nick?" Johnnie asked. "You wanna tell me what's going on?"

He waited a moment before speaking. "Are you with Anthony?"

"What's going on, Nick?" Johnnie asked in a firmer tone.

"Put me on the speaker. He needs to hear this too." He was already on the speaker and totally disregarded Johnnie's question a second time.

"I'm here," I said.

"And I'm very disappointed in you guys. You should be dead by now. But you just had to leave the house. Well let me make this short and to the point. If you care about Marco's life and the life of Jena, you will leave town and never return. Do you understand?

"Everything I've done was to create a new day in DC. There's a bigger picture here that neither of you can appreciate. I'll let your loved ones live, but you two have gotta go.

"And just so that the seriousness of the situation is clear, Anthony, I also have Coco. I'm not playing with you two."

"I'm sorry, what did you say?!" I said into the phone. "You have *both* of the girls?!"

"Yes." He said. "And if you want them to live, then leave. And don't ever look back. As for Marco, I'm sitting here with him right now."

"If you touch my father..." Johnnie yelled.

"Save your empty threats, boy! No one's scared of you. Besides, Marco is no longer relevant. Even if he wakes up from this coma, there's nothing he can do to stop me now. But you two, on the other hand...well, I just don't want to risk it.

"So I'll say it again. Leave town. If you don't, the girls die. If you challenge me, I come back here and smother Marco for the hell of it. You can't win. Just go."

Johnnie looked to Marty, who was now sitting Indian style, listening to the conversation. His smugness made Johnnie sick. He had the "*I told you so*" look plastered across his face.

I could tell this was making Johnnie angry. We had confirmation. The man entrusted with his families' safety had been plotting against them the entire time.

"We're not going anywhere," Johnnie said.

"Well, the consequences have been made clear. And if you don't like it, you'll know where to find me."

Nick Nick didn't wait for a response. He hung up the phone. And Marty didn't wait to be invited into the discussion, he launched into giving us his two cents.

"I told you he was a snake! Untie me and let's go get that bastard! You know he's going to kill those girls no matter what you do. Let's get him!"

Johnnie stared at his phone like he was expecting it to ring again. But he knew it wouldn't, he was deep in thought. "You're right." He didn't want to, but he now accepted that Nick Nick was capable of doing anything. And if he were able to orchestrate a house fire that eliminated all of the criminal competition, then killing Coco and his sister would be a walk in the park.

"Ok! Then let's go!" Marty struggled to his feet. "See. I told you we had nothing to do with the hit on Humpty."

"Yup." Johnnie said with a hint of condescension that didn't register with Marty. But it registered with me. And I knew exactly where he was going with it. "You're absolutely right. You had nothing to do with the hit on Humpty." Since the first flare had burned to ground,

Johnnie pulled a second one from his back pocket. "But what about the hit on Anthony?"

"Huh? Whaaa?" A befuddled Marty replied. "What...what, what do you mean?"

"What do I mean?" Johnnie said mockingly. He stuck up the flare. "There were two hits that night and you spent this whole time telling us you had nothing to do with the one on Humpty, but I find it hard to believe you and your boss hadn't already decided to eliminate Anthony. Just in case you're ultimate takeover of my father's business didn't go the way you expected it.

"I get it...you was banking on Nick Nick destroying everything from the inside and then you'd come in and pounce from the outside. But you needed to make sure that Anthony was gone first. It was just a freak coincidence that the hits happened on the same night, wasn't it?

"You tried to kill my brother, Marty. He was the 'errand boy' Oronzio wanted out of the way. And I can't let that slide."

"Wait," Marty begged. "Wait!"

But it was too late. The lit flare had been tossed. The fuel ignited in a burst of flames. Marty's body dropped to the ground in an effort to roll the flames out, but he only landed on a ground that was oversaturated with gasoline. The flames grew higher. He screamed in agony.

We didn't wait for the screams to end or the body to stop writhing on the ground. Johnnie grabbed Marty's hatchets. "I'll take good care of these."

Nick Nick's final word hung in my head, "...you know where to find me." We hopped back in Marty's car because we knew exactly what Nick Nick meant. He was waiting for us, back at Marco's Restaurant.

Chapter 63

Nick Nick stood over Marco's motionless body in the hospital room. He patted him on the arm. "It would probably be best for you to stay asleep, my good friend. Your boys are without a doubt going to die tonight. We have so many years between us and I would hate to put you in the ground too. So stay asleep. You've worked so hard and deserve the rest."

Nick Nick bent over and gave Marco a brotherly kiss on his forehead. "Farewell, my friend."

Nick Nick walked to the door. It was time for him to leave Marco, for what he hoped would be the last time. But before he could make it into the hallway, he had an epiphany.

He searched up and down the hallway for the nearest doctor or nurse. Considering the late hour he was confident that no one was around.

Nick Nick walked back into Marco's hospital room. He shut and locked the door behind him. "You know what?" Nick Nick asked. "So long as you're alive, I'll never be able to truly run this town. Everyone will seek you out. They'll defer to you before following me."

Nick Nick wanted full control. He regretted it, but knew what he needed to do. There was an extra pillow in the chair, next to the bed. He grabbed it before pulling the breathing tube out of Marco's mouth.

Marco made an involuntary gasp for air. Nick Nick fixed the pillow over Marco's face. All he had to do was apply pressure. He pushed. And he pushed some more.

After awhile, the incessant beeping of the heart monitor sang a steady tone.

Marco Ribisi was dead.

Chapter 64

There was a dark figure standing at the end of the alley as we drove up in Marty Fucker's car. The headlights crept along the cemented driveway until they reached his feet.

After killing the engine and turning the lights off, both Johnnie and I jumped out. I was hoping that we didn't bring any unneeded attention to the alley that was situated across from the restaurant.

The dark figure was Smitty. Since calling and telling me about his earlier experience, I asked him to stay there until we arrived. Guilt-ridden, he was more than willing to do it. "Geez. I'm sorry guys. I had no idea."

"It's not your fault," I said. "Nobody knew."

"It didn't hit me that something was off until they took Jena from me. Nick Nick rushed me outta there. That's when I called you."

Johnnie spoke up for the first time. "You heard Anthony. It's not your fault. We have to play the hand we're dealt." Johnnie grasped Smitty's hand and held it firmly. "We've got work to do."

Hearing this made Smitty feel much better about the situation. To think that he hand delivered Johnnie's sister to a murderous fate had been eating him up inside.

I also wanted to take a minute to appreciate Johnnie's maturity, but we didn't have the time. Even Johnnie sensed the need for speed and a sense of urgency.

Without skipping a beat, Johnnie asked, "So what have we missed?"

"It's been busy," Smitty said. "Men coming and going. Nick Nick has been in and out, but he's back now. I haven't seen the girls in a while, but as far as I can tell, they're both still inside. They're in your father's office. There was also a woman, with who I think was her bodyguard. He looked like a serious dude."

"I'll bet anything he's the guy from the video of Humpty's murder," I said.

While Smitty was breaking down the early morning events to Johnnie, I kept watch on the front door, hoping to catch a glimpse of the girls. I saw one of the men who chased us in Union Station earlier. I saw Nick Nick come to the front door and hold a brief conversation with him. And then twenty seconds into their talk, I saw an unexpected face walk out of the restaurant and join the discussion.

"What the fuck! Is that who I think it is?"

Johnnie and Smitty whipped their heads in my direction. Johnnie didn't know what was going on. "Well who is it?"

"Oh yeah..." Smitty said. "And then there's that. Detective Sam Daniels. We were on the force together and there were always rumors that he was dirty. Guess there's no doubt now."

The family always knew Nick Nick had connections with the police. I just didn't think he had anyone brazen enough to be a part of a scheme, like the one he had been hatching. The other thing that had my mind spinning was that Detective Daniels' partner had been trying to get me to talk with him about organized crime for years.

The irony. While Aguilar had been working to put Marco and Nick Nick behind bars, Daniels was working to keep Nick Nick in business. This gave me an idea that could potentially bring this madness to an end.

"This changes things." I patted my pants pockets in search of my wallet. Once I found it, I pulled out a few business cards that I've kept from different people I met over the years.

Shuffling through them, I finally found the one I had been looking for. I grabbed my cell phone and dialed. Even though I was preoccupied, I could hear Smitty giving Johnnie more background information on Detective Daniels.

"Yes, I'll hold." I said into the phone. I only waited another few seconds before I was forwarded to his personal cell phone and he was on the other end. "Detective Aguilar. It's Anthony Ribisi. We need to meet."

Chapter 65

"You're out of your fucking mind, Nick Nick!" Daniels was livid.

Nick Nick was a block of ice, with his back against the bar. Daniels paced back and forth, in front of him.

Nick Nick wasn't concerned. He merely offered a warning. "Be careful."

"Careful? You must be joking! Were you careful when you burned down a house full of people? And what about those girls back there?" he said, pointing to Marco's office. "Were you careful when you decided to add kidnapping to the mix? We're well beyond being careful!"

The yelling caught the attention of Malak, who had been standing at the door, outside of Marco's office. The commotion caused him to walk into the bar area and watch what he thought was certain to be great entertainment.

Navy blue suit guy had also heard the uproar. He abandoned his post to run inside and see what all the fuss was about.

Still a bit frosty, Nick Nick said, "It's not your concern. Don't worry about it."

"This must be a joke," Daniels said, incredulously. "That's it. You're joking. You're a big fucking joke. But this shit ain't funny. Let me let you in on a little secret, and tell you how this works.

"If there's a fire, the fire department will determine whether it's accidental or intentionally set. If it's accidental, everyone goes their separate way, because shit happens. But if it's intentional, then the cops get involved, you dumb fuck."

At the sound of that last insult, Malak and navy blue suit guy looked at each other from across the room. Malak shook his head. The two decided it was best for them to mind their own business. They retreated to where they were originally posted.

From his location, Malak could see Marina standing in the kitchen, eavesdropping. She knew better than to interrupt Daniels and Nick Nick. Or better yet, she knew not to interrupt Nick Nick.

"We can't have the cops looking into what happened tonight!" Daniels yelled.

"But you are the cops. Contain it," Nick Nick said calmly.

"I can't control this!" Daniels erupted. He was now standing less than a foot away from Nick Nick. "An accidental fire, then fine! But your dumb ass chained the doors! You chained the fuckin' doors!

"Fire chief, police chief, homicide AND the organized crime units...everyone's hand up the bitch's skirt, feeling around for some pussy. Even the God damn mayor!"

Daniels stopped his tirade. He stepped even closer to Nick Nick. He seemed as if he calmed down, or at least he was exhausted. But it was only for a moment. He erupted again. "I can't contain a chained house full of french-fried mobsters!"

"I told you to be careful." Nick Nick sighed.

"Fuck you, Nick Nick. I'm done with you. After tonight, find someone else to put on your payroll. Give me a couple dollars and you think you own me. You can kiss my ass."

Still as calm and collected as ever, Nick Nick said, "Find someone else, you say?" And with lightening quick speed, Nick Nick threw a fist at Daniels' throat. He could feel the man's Adam's apple collapse behind the weight of his knuckles.

This caused Daniels to immediately bend over in excruciating pain. He grabbed his neck, coughing uncontrollably. Before Daniels could maneuver away, compose himself, or launch a counter attack, Nick Nick grabbed him by the neck with his right hand and freed the gun out of his Daniels' holster, with his left.

Nick Nick led Daniels to a chair, slamming the coughing man down in it. He tightened the grip on his neck. With a crushing blow, Nick Nick slammed the butt of Daniels' gun against his jaw. The force caused Daniels to fly out of the chair and hit the floor.

He picked Daniels up by the neck again and threw him against the bar. Daniels must have flown seven feet across the room. Nick Nick watched Daniels as he struggled to get to his feet. He approached the disoriented man and grabbed him by his collar.

Disregarding the blood trickling from a gash on Daniels' cheek, Nick Nick struck him with the gun again. This time, not allowing him to go anywhere, Nick Nick slammed Daniels on the bar, face down.

He leaned over and whispered into Daniels' ear. "Now let me let *you* in on a little secret, and tell you how this works. I don't give a fuck if the head of the FBI, CIA and Jesus Christ was investigating that fire...your job is to do what I tell you to do. Contain it. You got me."

Nick Nick waited for a response, but all he could hear was coughing. "I don't hear you."

Daniels was in no condition to use his throat for anything other than coughing. He feverishly nodded his head up and down to indicate that he heard Nick Nick. It hurt like hell.

"Good." Nick Nick let go of Daniels and took a couple of steps away from him. Daniels pried himself off the bar top. A puddle of blood was left, along with an imprint of his cheek. "Now clean yourself up. Take the girls back to the house and wait for me. You parked in the alley?"

Daniels nodded.

"Good. Take the back way. I'm expecting Johnnie and Anthony to be here soon and I don't want them to see the girls leave."

Daniels composed himself as best as he could and then began walking back to Marco's office to retrieve Jena and Coco. But before he could exit the bar area, Nick Nick grabbed his attention again.

"I'm sorry. What was I thinking?" Nick Nick walked up to Daniels, gripped him by his wrist and thrust his gun into his open palm. "This belongs to you. You might need it tonight."

Daniels held his gun and attempted to walk away again. But Nick Nick hadn't released his wrist. "Contrary to what you think," Nick Nick said. "I do own you. Now go on. And be careful."

If Daniels had a tail, it would've been curled up under the backside of his body. He couldn't do anything, but walk away.

Chapter 66

"Where is this cop at?" Smitty asked me.

"He said he wouldn't be long." I looked at Johnnie and could tell he wasn't thrilled about the idea of calling the police. "I think this is the best move."

"Have you ever met a cop you trusted?" Johnnie asked.

"Well, I trust Smitty."

"Yeah, but I'm an ex-cop. Why do you think that is?" Smitty said. His tone sounded as if he was leaning more toward Johnnie's line of thinking than mine.

"Look. This guy has been gunning for Marco for the longest. Why not give him Nick Nick? If he bags Nick Nick and his crew, then he'll leave your father alone."

"Well, I don't like it. And I damn sure don't trust it," Johnnie said. "Besides, if he doesn't get here soon, then he won't get anybody."

Johnnie was absolutely right in that respect. We had no idea of what was going on inside the restaurant. If we waited too long, we ran the risk of missing our chance to rescue Coco and Jena. And the longer Aguilar took to get to us, there was also a greater chance that Nick Nick would get away.

Smitty spoke up. "This is taking too long."

"He's right," Johnnie said.

"Well, what do you suggest we do?" I was becoming impatient with their impatience.

"We go with plan B. Which was really plan A."

"Let's wait another fifteen minutes. I'm sure he'll be here by then."

"No fuckin' way. We can't wait any longer! We've come here to get a job done. You can sit here if you want."

"Plan B, huh? You sure you wanna do that?" I asked.

"Abso-fuckin-lutely." Johnnie was determined. He was focused. He didn't want to let another minute slip by without acting.

"Ok," I said. Then I turned toward Smitty. "You remember what you have to do right?" But before I could finish the question, he had already dashed out of the alley and made a beeline to his right.

He was careful not to be seen by the man in the navy blue suit, standing guard, at the restaurant. I did the same, exiting to my left, and Johnnie got into the driver's seat of Marty Fucker's car.

As I moved away from the alley, I could hear the engine crank. Smitty and I were briskly walking in opposite directions, leaving Johnnie alone in the alley. My hope was that he wouldn't do anything dumb. Keep his head and stick to the script.

A man could hope.

Chapter 67

Coco and Jena sat in Marco's office in silence. They faced each other in their chairs, looking almost like mirror images. Legs crossed. Arms crossed over their chest.

Occasionally they could hear muted sounds from the other side of the closed door. But nothing loud enough for them to put together what was going on. So they sat there. Staring at one another. In silence.

Coco was the first to break the quiet. "What the hell is going on?"

Jena heard the question, but wasn't sure how to respond. Any other time, she would think of some witty retort that was constructed to answer the question, but not give insight to her family.

She was skilled at the art of dancing around a question. But in this case, the music had stopped. She had two left feet. She couldn't see a dance partner. It was like she stood alone in the middle of a dance floor. Lost.

But Coco was intent on getting answers. "Excuse me." She said, leaning forward and breaking the mirror image. "Do you mind telling me what's going on?"

Jena could only answer the question with honesty. It was all she had left. "I don't know."

The sound of keys bouncing against a door jolted Jena out of her daze. Not knowing what to do, both of the women leapt out of their seats and approached the door. Once it opened, a look of relief came across Jena's face. But Coco was still confused.

"Thank God!" Jena said, eyeing Daniels. "He's a cop." She said to Coco. She was so happy to see a familiar face. If the man was sent to the hospital to protect her father, then surely he would do the same for her, she thought

She was excited. Coco wasn't.

The man looked disheveled. Not to mention, he was holding a white cloth napkin to the side of his face. There was blood all over it. Coco was far from excited.

Jena was so concerned for her own wellbeing that thoughts of her father's safety didn't immediately register. But it didn't take long to hit her.

"Wait a minute. Why aren't you at the hospital?"

Daniels pointed at Coco. "You. Let's go."

Still a bit confused, Coco started taking small steps toward Daniels. That is, until Jena blocked her path and held her back by the arm. "Hold on…" Jena said to Coco.

"But you said he was a cop, right?"

Jena didn't acknowledge Coco's question. Instead, her daze was dissipating, and clarity was returning. "Where's my father, detective?" she asked.

Daniels' patience was wearing thin. He tossed the napkin to the ground, unveiling an ugly gash across his cheek. He then pulled his gun from his holster. "I don't have time for this." Waving his gun, as if it was an extension of his hand and he was beckoning a friend to come closer, he shook his head side-to-side and said "Come here!"

Neither girl moved.

Daniels rushed over to the girls and grabbed Coco by her free arm and started walking out of the room. Jena held on to Coco's other arm tighter. Coco let out a slight scream, as she was stretch between the two.

Without a second thought Daniels doubled back and pushed his gun into Jena's forehead. Her instinct was to drop Coco's arm and raise her hands high.

"You think I won't kill you?" Daniels said.

"I'm sorry! I'm sorry!" Jena cried out. "But where are you taking her?"

"Don't you worry. She isn't going alone. I'll be back for you in a minute."

Daniels tugged Coco by the arm and headed out the office, making sure that the door was locked behind him. He headed a few feet down a narrow hallway and exited through the back door, ending up in the back alley.

Baldie was on guard at that door. Aside from the huge green dumpster, the only other thing in the alley was Daniels' car. He paid no attention to Baldie, completely ignoring the brushing of shoulders as he darted out of the building.

The detective yanked the back driver side door open and tossed Coco inside. He climbed in after and pushed her over to the passenger side. By that time, he had his handcuffs out of his pocket.

"Give me your wrists!" he demanded. Coco put up a little resistance, but it was of no use. Daniels cuffed her to a bar that was welded into the door.

Daniels backed out of the open car door. When he finally stood straight, he turned around and acknowledged Baldie for the first time. Though it was only eye contact, it was still acknowledgment.

"You having a rough a day?" Baldie sarcastically asked.

By then, Daniels was already on his way back into the restaurant. "Fuck you," was the only response he could muster.

For the time being, Daniels was focused on finishing his job for Nick Nick. Despite what Nick Nick said, Daniels was done with him. *Finish this last job*, he thought to himself. He had enough. *Finish this last job*, he thought again.

With Coco secured in the vehicle, it was time to get Jena.

Chapter 68

Smitty quickly and carefully walked toward the end of the block. Stealth was his main objective. Make it to the alley that was perpendicular to U Street without being noticed by the man in navy blue. The surrounding early morning darkness made it easy.

He made it to his mark and then scurried across the street. Smitty was far enough away from the posted sentinel, but he didn't want to take the chance that a lazy stroll would get him spotted. Once in the alley, he stepped as quietly as he could, making his way to the intersection of another alleyway that would bring him closer to the back entrance of the restaurant.

His eyes adjusted enough to see Daniels struggling with Coco in the backseat. *This motherfucker better not hurt her*, he thought. As soon as Daniels darted back into the building, Smitty's first instinct was to run to the car and grab Coco, but then he saw Daniels pass another man. The bald guy was clearly on the lookout, in the back of the building, like the one in the front. This kept Smitty in the shadows.

He knew that in order to get to Coco before Daniels returned, he would need to take care of the bald guy, and quick. *I need a diversion.* He looked beyond the man standing at the door and saw a trash dumpster on the other side of him. That gave him an idea.

Find a bottle. Find a bottle. Find a bottle.

"Quick! They're always lying around in alleys." But none was to be found. "Damn! This is the cleanest alley ever!" Smitty whispered. And then he saw one. It was standing upright, a few inches from the wall across from him. The only problem was that it was right behind Daniels' car. The bigger problem...Daniels' car was five feet away from Baldie.

How the hell was he going to get to it without being seen? In the meantime he clung to the darkness against the wall. Praying he was sufficiently hidden. Praying even harder he could make his move before Daniels returned.

Baldie paced back and forth. Walking closer to the car and then walking away, in the direction of the dumpster, and then back toward the car. In his back and forth, a scurrying sound of tiny paws caught his attention. Smitty couldn't see what it was, but he heard it as well. Probably a rat. DC alleys are notorious for its vermin population. Or it could've been a stray cat. Baldie wasn't sure what to make of it, so he walked closer to the dumpster.

While his back was turned, Smitty made his move. He dashed as quietly as possible and crouched behind the rear bumper of Daniels' car. Baldie never saw him.

With the bottle now in hand, and still surrounded by a good amount of darkness, Smitty looked to perfectly time his next move. And just before Baldie turned around to make it back to the car, Smitty lobbed the glass bottle in the air.

It had a high enough arch that it flew well above Baldie's bald head. And it hung long enough in the air that he was able to walk back to his post before the bottle landed and shattered on the concrete ground.

The sound of the bottle splintering into countess pieces startled the bald man way more than the shuffling of rat paws. He jerked his head toward the dumpster, whipped out his pistol, and quickly marched back in that direction.

He was moving fast. But Smitty was a bigger and swifter beast. He moved faster. And before Baldie knew what was going on, Smitty had the back of his bald head in the palm of his hand.

Smitty slammed the man's face into the green dumpster. Then he slammed it again. The gun flew out of Baldie's hand. For good measure, Smitty lifted the man off of his feet and body slammed him onto the pavement. He then straddled the nearly unconscious man and shattered his jaw, with a rock solid fist.

Baldie was out for the count.

Smitty grabbed the gun, which was a few feet away, and then raced to the open car door. All of the commotion had Coco scared to death. She backed up against the locked door in an effort to get away from Smitty.

"Don't be afraid, princess. I'm getting you out of here," Smitty said.

"But...but...what about Jena?" Coco said as Smitty climbed in the back seat. He took a minute to examine the handcuffs.

"Look." He spoke through gritted teeth. "My purpose is to take out who I can, rescue who I can, and then get the hell out of Dodge. And that's what we're going to do." Frustrated with the cuffs, he said, "Hold on."

Smitty ran back to the unconscious man and searched through all of his pockets. He couldn't find keys to the handcuffs. "Fuck!" he said loud enough for Coco to hear.

Smitty ran back to the car and took another look at the keyhole on the handcuffs. He then leaned over the seats and started rummaging through the ashtray, glove box, and small compartment.

"What are you doing?" Coco asked.

"It's been awhile since I picked a lock. I'm looking for something I can use."

Coco felt a surge of excitement. "I've heard about bobby pins. Do bobby pins work?!"

"Oh my God. Why didn't you say you had one?"

Coco had taken a bobby pin out of her hair and handed it to Smitty. He twisted it back and forth at the bend, until it was broken in two pieces. Working the broken edge of the pin, he fumbled around without success.

An anxious Coco pleaded with Smitty. "Hurry!"

"I told you..." Smitty said as they then both heard the sound of a click. "...it's been a while."

Smitty carefully backed out of the car and led Coco by her hands. *I'm finally safe*, she thought, until Smitty was fully out of the vehicle. When he turned around to take her out of the alley, they were both pained to see Detective Daniels in the doorway of the building behind them.

He had Jena by the arm. He also held a gun to her head.

"Make another move, and I blow her brains out."

Chapter 69

I never noticed how peaceful U Street was at four in the morning. It felt like I was in a small crease of time where the late night activities of the area had been put to bed, and there was an obligatory moment of silence before the next day could begin.

There wasn't a soul out or a car on the road. It was urban tranquility at its best. Almost like the area paused for prayer.

I was amazed that the man in the navy blue suit hadn't noticed Smitty or I creeping down U Street, in opposite directions. I was thankful because that meant the element of surprise was still on our side.

Well, at least it was for a little while longer. It was my aim to make our presence known, fairly quickly.

I could see the man standing guard, but I was far enough down the sidewalk that he couldn't see me. Facing him, I could finally admit, there was a hatred taking over. There was uncertainty regarding Marco. Both Jena and Coco were being held hostage, or already dead. And all that I had worked for and known since I was a young boy had been burned to the ground.

Succumbing to the intensity of emotions was unchartered territory. I prided myself on being a careful man who acted on planning, discipline, and measured calculation. But here I was, standing on a desolate street corner, with water brimmed at the bottom of my eyes.

My body was on autopilot. My mind had relinquished control. I walked slowly toward the restaurant. I floated actually because I couldn't feel my feet moving.

I must have been halfway to the man standing out front before he noticed someone moving in his direction. And once he did, we were both facing each other. He didn't move. He just stared.

I think he was trying to figure out if I was who he thought I was. And then it hit him. *He had eyes on Anthony Ribisi.* Now we were both moving toward each other.

That's when I decided to pick up my pace. I found myself in a light jog. He walked briskly, with a sense of urgency. I could see him motion to his waistband with his right hand and slightly brush his jacket back. He wanted easy access to his gun. He must have known he would need it.

By now, I was in full sprint and we were approximately thirty yards away from each other. My attention was fully centered on him. And it had to be. He had drawn his gun and I wasn't a bullet dodger, by any means. As difficult as it was, I needed to be focused.

Fifty feet stood between us. And even though my eyes were locked on him, out of my periphery, I could see a car cut across the street, in the direction of the restaurant. The nearly three thousand pound vehicle jumped the curb and went crashing into the glass façade of Marco's Restaurant.

The sound of metal warping and glass crunching startled the man in the navy blue suit. His reaction time was less than a second. His face resembled a man under the attack of firepower and bombs. He threw his body on the concrete at the sound of the collision and spun around toward the wreckage.

His gun had already been in hand. Instinctively, he squeezed the trigger, spitting bullets in the direction of the car. He must have dumped half of his clip before he saw that the car was empty.

But it was still running, the door was open, and there was a metal pipe jammed between the driver's seat and the throttle. The car had been sent across the street on autopilot.

Before he could realize the mistake of his involuntary movement, I was on him. The barrel of my gun was pressed against the back of his head. I never stopped running toward him. One shot was all it took. His head exploded. His body was limp on the ground.

Johnnie peeked out of the alley to make sure it was safe for him to move. I pointed to the back of the sputtering car. He knew what I meant.

Johnnie darted across the street and ducked low behind his improvised battering ram. I met him in a matter of seconds. Johnnie quickly peeked over the car's roof and then came back. "Coast is clear. Brother. You ready?" Without waiting for a reply, he looked at me and then said, "Yeah. You're ready."

Understanding that the light work had already been handled, there was no anxiety. We both had our guns drawn, and took the calmest walk into hell that had ever been taken.

Chapter 70

Inside Marco's office, Nick Nick sat at Marco's desk. He completely owned the space now. Like it had been his the whole time. Malak stood in front of the desk and Marina sat on its top.

"You sure they're going to come?" she asked.

"As sure as water is wet. They'll be here. It's just a matter of when. And if we'll be ready."

"We're ready," she reassured him.

"Should I handle the girls?" Malak asked.

"No... I'll need you to help me deal with Johnnie and Anthony. Our men should be taking the girls to the house right now. Once the boys are out of the way, then we'll kill the girls. No one should be left alive. But we need to do it in phases.

"After that, we'll lay low for a few weeks. With all the competition dead, the streets will run wild for a little bit. It'll feel like the streets of Iraq, after the American invasion. They'll be no direction. A whole bunch of Indians trying to be chief...foot soldiers playing like they're generals. And at the point when it looks like everything is in utter chaos, I'll open the gambling houses again. Mary, you'll gather the ladies and put them back on the street.

Malak...you'll go business to business, convincing them all why they need protection from people like me. I have someone coming in to run the drug game and I'll run double duty cleaning the money.

"Wherever there's money, that's where we'll be. Let them jump start the game and then we'll muscle them out. And what's the competition going to do? Nothing. They can't beat us. It'll be a brand new DC. And we'll run this town. Like a real family should."

Marina liked the sound of Nick Nick's plan. She grabbed the hands of both men and said, "I'm so happy our family could finally be together."

Malak on the other hand, pursed his lips and furrowed his brow. "The drugs," he said. "...someone new?"

Nick Nick cracked a smile. "Well...not new to everybody."

Marina and Malak looked at each other, not knowing what to make of what Nick Nick said.

The puzzled look on their faces only lasted a moment. As soon as Nick Nick uttered his cryptic words, the building shook. The crash of glass was so loud that it sounded like a window exploded in the very room where they stood.

Nick Nick and Marina jumped to their feet. Malak quickly ran to the door, cracked it open and stuck his head out. All he saw was a car sitting in the dining room. The engine was still running. But over the sound of the engine, he heard gunfire. It sounded like bullets were hitting the car. Then he heard one last single gunshot over the humming of the still running car engine.

When he pulled himself back into the room, Nick Nick had already fished out his firearm and was checking to ensure it was loaded. "They're here," Malak calmly said.

"Like I said...as water is wet. Tonight we give birth to a new city. You ready for it?"

Malak, ever calm and collected, only nodded his head up and down.

"Do you have a gun?" Nick Nick asked.

Malak shook his head side to side and pulled his jacket back to expose the sheathed machete that he loved so much. It hung in a holster under his left arm. "No need."

"Then let's go," Nick Nick said. Malak was eager to get the festivities started. He was already out the door. Nick Nick turned to Marina. "Stay here until the shooting stops. Don't leave this room unless there's complete silence, and not a moment before."

Nick Nick kissed Marina with passion. He only exhibited this kind of emotion when he was with her. Then as quickly as Malak had dashed through the door, Nick Nick did the same.

Marina sat at Marco's desk. She opened all of the drawers and felt around until she found what she was looking for. "Of course he would have one." She pulled out a tiny black Smith and Wesson six shot revolver. She clasped it between her small hands. She sat upright. And she waited.

"Come in here if you want, motherfucker," she said. "I've got something for you."

* * *

Running out of the office, Malak crept down the left side of the decimated room. There was glass everywhere. Tables and chairs had been knocked down. Porcelain dishware had been broken into homemade jigsaw puzzles and they were scattered throughout the dining room. The room was a mess. Not to mention the running car leaning across the windowsill.

Hoping to keep the element of surprise, Malak slithered into the room.

Nick Nick, on the other hand, was a different animal all together. He walked to the middle of the monsoon stricken room and stood there. He saw Johnnie peep from above the car roof, but Johnnie didn't notice him.

"Come on. I'm right here," Nick Nick whispered.

Chapter 71

"Now!" Johnnie yelled.

He and I ran into the restaurant along the left hand side of the car. As soon as we entered the dining room, we could see Nick Nick standing there, waiting for us. I thought the coast was clear. But I was wrong.

There he was, gun extended and raining bullets down on Johnnie and me. We dove to the ground, splitting in two different directions.

I felt bullets fly past my head. Once Johnnie and I split, it seemed like Nick Nick made his choice. Shoot me first. Johnnie could see it too, so he didn't hesitate. He took advantage of the opportunity and began firing back at Nick Nick.

Nick Nick was a standing target. He wizened up and dove for cover, now shooting in Johnnie's direction. I popped up and shot at Nick Nick, hoping I would be able to hit him and bring all of this to an end.

Bullets were everywhere, but nobody was being hit. What a waste of ammunition. All three of us shielded ourselves pretty well. So for the moment, no bullets were being shot.

"Anthony!" Nick Nick yelled out to me. "Let's stop this! Put a bullet in Johnnie and come work for me! Johnnie always was a fuck up anyway! Kill that little bitch and let's get to work!"

Divide and conquer was hard at work here. "You can kiss my ass, Nick Nick!" I yelled back. "If you really want me to kill something, why don't you step out in the open?!'

"Yeah! Come out where we can see you!" Johnnie added.

"Nobody's talking to you!" Nick Nick quickly shot back. "Let the adults talk, you fucking baby! You know he'll only hold you back Anthony! I'm taking over the city and you can be right there with me. Almost like father and son. I was more of a father to you than Marco ever was.

"Who taught you the rules of the business? Me! I trained you in every skill you have. Who took you out on your first kill? Taught you how to dispose of bodies? Get the grime of blood from under your fingernails? It was all me!

"You're not a mini-Marco. Face it boy, you're a mini-Nick Nick. Now put a bullet in Johnnie and let's own this town!"

"Mini-Nick Nick?! You must be crazy!" I said. "I would never sell out my people for my own gain. I'm nothing like you! Everything I learned about the business and how to do it, I learned from Marco. Not you!"

"Really? And how's that working out for you? Hopefully better that it worked out for Marco. Keep on believing you're just like him, and you'll be DEAD! Just like him!"

My blood boiled at the thought of Marco's death. Then I looked at Johnnie. If my blood was boiling, he was ready to explode.

Chapter 72

Smitty took three side steps to his left. If Daniels was to start shooting, he thought that stepping away from the girl was a good idea. And it worked. Daniels took his gun away from Jena and pointed at the hulk of a man, giving no thought to Coco either.

"Hey, Sammy. It's been a long time," Smitty said sarcastically.

"Yeah. It has. But don't take another step. They'll die if you do." Daniels stepped over the lifeless man on the ground. Dragging Jena over him as well.

"You got it. It's your world, man." Smitty's hands were raised way above his head.

"And I know you probably have his gun," Daniels said, motioning to the bald man. "Why don't you take it from wherever you've tucked it, and slide it over here? Slowly."

Making deliberate movements, Smitty reached into his waistband and pulled out the gun...dangling it between his thumb and index finger. He placed the gun on the ground and kicked it over to the detective.

Daniels flashed a huge grin and said, "Gooood." He reveled at the thought of being in control. He pulled out a second pair of handcuffs, shoved them into Jena's hand,

and threw her toward Smitty. "Put the bitches in the car and cuff them together."

Smitty's mind raced a mile a minute. He took time to observe his surroundings. The cramped alley didn't leave him many options. Especially with a gun aimed directly at him. Any rash move would guarantee their death in a hail of bullets.

Even though he didn't want to, he had to do it. He grabbed Jena and Coco by their arms and led them to the car. The look of despair on the faces of both of the girls was apparent. "Noooo. Don't do this." Jena whispered, as she was being tethered to Coco. Coco was crying again.

"I don't have a choice," he whispered back. "But don't worry." Smitty placed the girls in the car and then turned to face Daniels. "Nick Nick's bitch, huh? Never thought I'd see the day."

"And who are you calling a bitch? You're a fucking bouncer at a shitty nightclub. I never thought I'd see *that* day. At least I'm paid well for being someone's hoe."

Instead of walking away from the car, Smitty began taking slow steps toward Daniels. And Daniels noticed.

"Stop right where you are, or you're a dead man," Daniels said. But by that time, he was within arm's reach, which was exactly where Smitty wanted him.

Smitty prided himself on his ability to take advantage of opportunities as they became available. And he was expecting an opportunity to present itself shortly. He anticipated mayhem.

His internal clock told him that it was almost time for a conflict. He was expecting that Nick Nick would be confronted by the boys. That part of the plan never left his mind.

The expectation was for a car to go through the front of the restaurant. People would scatter. There would be a battle. Nick Nick would be on the losing end. And of course, being the rat that he was, he would then use the back door to abandon his sinking ship.

That was how he anticipated things would play out. At least as a best case scenario. But as Smitty stood there, staring down the barrel of Daniels' gun, he felt like he was waiting too long for everything to unfold. He started to doubt.

Plans change, of course. His part of the plan had him acquiring the girls and leaving. He wasn't supposed to be held at gunpoint in the alley. Plans do change.

"This little reunion was nice. Really, it was. But it's time for me the leave. Do you mind stepping to the side so we can be on our way," Daniels said.

Defeat washed over Smitty. He knew he couldn't stop Daniels. Especially without a gun. Letting him get into the car meant death for he and the girls.

But what could he do? Daniels was just as big and he was armed. Normally, that wouldn't matter. But in such tight quarters and with a gun aimed at him, he could only act at the right time. And if that time didn't present itself, then he was at a loss.

But then, it did. BL'DAT! – BL'DAT! – BLAP! – BLAP! – BLAP!

Gunfire! Smitty expected it at some point, so it didn't come as a complete surprise. But the erupting gunplay caught Daniels off guard just long enough for Smitty to rush him.

Let's get it! Smitty thought as he knocked Daniels' gun arm off to the side. He threw a left punch and connected with Daniels' jaw. He then swung a right uppercut, landing it squarely on the chin. The combination sent Daniels stumbling backwards. He was dazed, but he wasn't out of it.

Daniels found himself on one knee, trying to gather his faculties. He had forgotten that he was still clenching the gun in his right hand. Once it dawned on him, he raised the gun. But before he could point it in Smitty's direction, Smitty hurled his body through the air, causing a clash of the titans.

They rolled on the ground and struggled for control of the weapon. Throughout this whole time, the girls worked feverishly to free themselves from the handcuffs, without success.

The two men rolled and punched and kicked and scuffled. It was literally a back alley brawl. This went on until there was a loud BANG! Both girls stopped and whipped their heads toward the direction of the sound.

Both men were motionless. After a few seconds, one began to move. After a few more seconds, both girls gasped in terror. The person now walking toward the car was Detective Daniels. Smitty's body was tossed to the side and lying face down on top of Baldie. It was a body pile. His blood stream stained his clothes, the body beneath him, and the asphalt.

"Now." Daniels said, pointing his gun at Jena and Coco. "Anybody else want a bullet?" The girls didn't respond. "Good. Because I'm getting fed up with this sh—"

That's when a cannon roared from behind him. His head exploded, sending fragments of his skull, flesh, and brain in every direction. When his body fell to the ground, both Jena and Coco were amazed to see a wearied Smitty.

He was holding the gun he had earlier kicked toward Daniels, in one hand. In the midst of the scuffle, it was forgotten about. His other hand was covering a bullet wound on the right side of his abdomen.

Smitty grabbed the handcuff keys from Daniels' body. He limped over to the car and freed the girls. "Come on. We gotta go."

"We need to go back in there and get my brother, and Anthony!" Jena protested.

"No. You hear that?" There were police sirens blaring off in the distance. "Those cars will be here in no time. And we don't know what side of the shield they're on. If we wait, only to find out they belong to Nick Nick, then we're all as good as dead. We've gotta go...and now."

His rationale for leaving was correct. Jena didn't continue to disagree. "Well at least, let me drive. With that wound, you're in no condition."

Smitty didn't bother fighting her. He slid into the back seat with Coco. Jena got behind the wheel and started up the car. She hit the throttle as hard as she could, and took off, toward safety.

Chapter 73

Marco. Dead. How did we know he was telling the truth? How did we know he wasn't just trying to get under our skin? Maybe he was trying to affect our judgment, and take advantage of it. Maybe he was being honest.

I've never known Nick Nick to bluff. Especially when it came to murder. If he wanted you dead, you were already in a casket and didn't know it. There's no way he would lie about murdering Marco. Just no way.

A hate-filled Johnnie was already on his feet, squeezing out round after round. Slugs ricocheted off of metal and wood; they found themselves embedded into anything they could penetrate.

Johnnie stood in the middle of the room, firing in the direction of a hidden Nick Nick. "Fuck you!" he cried out. "You son of a bitch!" He would break from pulling the trigger to yell out other choice words.

From my crouched position, I could see Johnnie. His anger had blinded him, once again. Shooting up the dining room that he never wanted to inherit looked almost cathartic. But the sadder truth was that there was no soothing the pain of his father's death. Johnnie was merely being destructive, for destruction's sake.

"Come on out, Nick Nick! Show yourself, you bastard!" More shots were fired. And then there was the sound of a click, with each pull of the trigger. His clip was empty.

At that sound, I popped my head up from where I had taken cover, only to see Nick Nick doing the same. And Johnnie hadn't budged.

Nick Nick yelled out, "Alright young man! Now it's my turn!" And without hesitation, he jumped out and fired on Johnnie. But like a madman, Johnnie stood his ground. He didn't move, duck, or dodge. I couldn't tell if it was shock, anger or stupidity, but Johnnie didn't move.

I did the only thing I could think of at the time. Diving toward Johnnie, I tackled him to the ground. In the process, I was able to let off three shots toward Nick Nick. He was so fixated on Johnnie and so certain that I would stay in hiding that he hadn't expected me to leap out and shoot. But I did, and I got lucky.

The first two shots went wide right. The third hit him in his left shoulder. The force of the blow twisted his body and he stumbled back. From the ground, I could see he was in agonizing pain.

So what did I do? I fired again. And again. And again.

I was a terrible shot. I missed him with every try. But it put him on the defensive. Nick Nick gathered himself and ran out the back door toward the hallway. I knew that hallway led to the back alley. He was trying to run away.

I would give chase in a minute, but with Nick Nick gone, I needed to coach Johnnie. "What were you thinking?" I wasn't looking for a response.

We both got to our feet but Johnnie looked like he was in a different world. "Johnnie!" I yelled. "I need you man! I know it hurts. But we've gotta get that bitch and I can't do it alone."

Johnnie looked around the dining room. It looked like he was reminiscing. This was the place we shared many childhood memories. We crafted dreams of our future and dared anyone to tell us they wouldn't come true.

The two of us shared the same pain. We stood in the middle of a place that had been the essential foundation of our development, and we witnessed it being destroyed. It wasn't just about bullets and broken glass. Or even the car through the window. It was instead about knowing that the structure of our family, which had been in place our whole lives, was now no more. Trust, faith, love, and loyalty...it was all gone.

And in spite of feeling the pain, I knew that above all, there could be retribution. But only if we were strong enough to look past our pain and act. This was the fundamental difference between Johnnie and I.

"Johnnie!" I said. "I'm going after him. Are you coming?"

Johnnie snapped out of his trance. "Yeah...yeah, I'm coming."

"Take a minute to breathe or do what you need to get your mind right. Only a minute. I don't want him getting too ahead of us."

"Thanks, man. That's all I'll need. I'll be right there."

And with that affirmation I ran out of the room. Glancing back briefly, I could see Johnnie walk over to the bar. He leaned against it and slid down until his behind was on the floor and his back was pressed on the wood. Johnnie hung his head.

I didn't like the sight of that. But one thing was for sure, I had to move forward. Nick Nick was on the run. And someone had to go after him.

I had to move forward.

Chapter 74

Johnnie watched a digital clock hanging across from him. One minute, he thought. He waited for the time to change. "Get your shit together. He's right. No time to be a bitch." And then the time changed. A minute had passed.

He took few deep breaths and looked at his gun that was lying on the floor. He knew it was empty. He even chuckled thinking, "How could I be so dumb?"

Johnnie hopped up and ran to the wrecked car. After snatching the door open, he placed his hand under the driver seat and searched around. "There you are." He had found it.

He needed another gun if he was going to join the party. Now that he had one, he ran back into the building to make his way to the alley.

He began running full speed. He dodged broken chairs and jumped over other debris. As soon as he got past the car, the surprise of his life was waiting for him. From behind a rectangular pillar, Malak jumped out, swinging the trunk of a broken table. Malak connected with Johnnie's chest.

Since Johnnie was already jumping through the air, the strength of the hit caused him to do a full back flip. Johnnie landed on his stomach.

Nearly unconscious, Johnnie was powerless against Malak's advance. Without wasting a moment, Malak pounced on Johnnie. Placing a knee on his back, he grabbed a fist full of Johnnie's hair.

"Where are you going?" Malak leaned over and whispered in Johnnie's ear. "You seemed to be in such a hurry. Why don't you just stick around and have some fun with me?"

Still dazed and pinned under Malak, all Johnnie could do was listen. Barely. Malak dug his knee deeper into Johnnie's back and he felt the back holster, which contained Johnnie's newly acquired axe. Being a man who loved to work with blades, he knew exactly what it was.

Malak unsheathed his machete. "What the hell is this?" he asked mockingly. He began ripping and slicing through Johnnie's light jacket and shirt to uncover the holster and axe. In the process, Malak opened up Johnnie's skin through a series of slashes across his back. Blood saturated his tattered clothes.

Malak snatched the axe from its holding place. "Do you even know what to do with that?" He tossed it across the room. "You probably don't."

Malak repositioned his hand over the back of Johnnie's neck and took a firm grip, holding him tightly against the floor. He placed his machete against Johnnie's cheek and slowly dragged the edge of the blade along the side of his face until the skin ruptured.

"You've got to have patience in order to use a blade. And I know all about you, Johnnie. Hot-headed. Brash.

Foolhardy. Impatient. You don't know how to wait. But me, on the other hand…I know how to hide in patience and wait for my moment. I've been here the whole time, Johnnie. I could have jumped out earlier, but what fun would that have been? I would've lost the chance to have this quality time with you. But I was patient. And here we are.

"That's what it's truly about, Johnnie. Practicing patience. It's a shame you'll never fully learn this lesson.

You think you're ready for that axe? You're not patient enough for it!"

Malak tightened his grip on Johnnie's hair. "No. You're not ready. But there is one thing you're certainly ready for…Death!"

Chapter 75

Crashing through the door to the alley, I saw Nick Nick shooting at a car, which was screeching away. I assumed Smitty was able to get the girls and make a run for it. I also noticed bodies littered throughout the alley. Smitty's handiwork? I was sure of it.

Trying to take advantage of the surprise element, I ran across the alley shooting in Nick Nick's direction. But even with the shoulder injury, he was still fast. He took cover behind a dumpster, which was really the only thing in the alley to hide behind.

Before Nick Nick could stick his hand out from behind the green shield and shoot back, I bounced off of the wall in front of me and headed back into the building. I stuck my arm out of the doors' portal and fired in the direction of the dumpster again. The sound of bullets hitting metal echoed. I could also hear police sirens coming our way.

I popped my head out to see if I was lucky enough to have hit Nick Nick. No such luck. He shot at me, but only hit the wall. Fragments of brick flew my way. That's when my luck changed.

Nick Nick continued to squeeze the trigger of his gun and the only thing that now echoed through the alley was *CLICK!* He was out of bullets.

Jumping back into the alley, I called for him. "Nick!" I yelled. "Come on out! It's over!"

"Over, huh?" Nick Nick said from his hiding spot. "Are you sure about that? I hear cops. Sounds like they'll be here in any minute. Once they get a look at these bodies, we'll both get locked up.

"This isn't over, boy. If we have to go inside, who do you think wins? This isn't over by a long shot. So why don't we do something more creative. Something a bit different. You go your way and I'll go mine. We can both avoid jail time. Having our freedom will give us a chance to finish this another day. What do you say?"

"Fuck you! That's what I say. Get your ass out here," I said, just as the sirens came to a stop. Red and blue lights filled the alley. "I'd risk going to jail if that means you'll be there too. And there ain't no guarantee you'll come out on top. You're only relevant if you're working. And when was the last time you put work in?"

Marco stepped out with his hands raised in the air. He tossed his empty gun on the ground. My gun was aimed at his chest. "Put work in?" he said "You mean, like when I killed Marco?"

He was trying to get under my skin. But it wasn't going to work. I wasn't Johnnie.

"Freeze!" I heard from behind. "Drop the gun!" The voice sounded like it belonged to Detective Aguilar. *Thank God*, I thought. Better late than never. But I still didn't lower my gun.

"Put the gun down, Anthony. Your job is done. You hear the other cars coming. This place will be swarming with cops soon. I can take it from here."

"He's got to pay," I said. "Jail is too good for him. He belongs in a ditch."

Aguilar pointed his gun at me. "Don't make any stupid decisions. Let me do what I've come here to do."

"He should be dead."

"I'm a cop! If you shoot him, then I have to take you in. Or shoot you. I don't want to do that. Anthony."

I didn't budge.

"*Jelani!* Just throw the gun over here. Nick Nick is finished."

I knew he was right. And I didn't want to go to jail for murdering Nick Nick. Even though he was the biggest scumbag I knew. And I didn't want to get shot either. I knew the best thing would have been for me to walk away and do something positive with the rest of my life. Marco had a plan to start a legitimate life; there was no reason why I couldn't.

I looked back at Aguilar for the first time. Nick Nick was frozen in place. I clenched the gun tighter than before. We were at a crossroads. One path took me to jail or the morgue. The other path was Aguilar arresting Nick Nick and giving *him* a one-way ticket to the penitentiary. I chose the latter.

There were sirens moving in closer to the entrance of the alley. I looked between Nick Nick and Aguilar, and heeding the detective's warning not to make any stupid decisions, I did what was right. I put the gun on safety and threw it toward the detective.

He picked up the gun with his free hand and stuffed it into his waistband. "That'a boy," he said to me. Then he asked, "What do you want me to do now?" But he wasn't talking to me. He was looking passed me, right at Nick Nick, who by this time, no longer had his hands raised.

Nick Nick, answered. "You know what to do. Kill this son of a bitch."

Chapter 76

The weight of Malak's hockey player frame was evenly distributed over Johnnie's body to the point where he could barely move or wiggle an inch. Johnnie's arm was pinned underneath his own body and the more he moved, the more his shoulder felt like it would rip out of its socket.

Even though the boy squirmed, this is exactly where Malak wanted him. He was completely under the big man's control, with nowhere to go. Death was inescapable.

"Are you ready to die, young Ribisi?" Malak asked.

"Fuck you!" Johnnie barked out. "If you're going to do it, get it over with!"

"Shhh..." Malak whispered into his ear. "What did I say about patience? I like to enjoy every moment, all the way until the blade pierces your back."

"My back?" Johnnie said, trying to push up against his captor. "What? You don't have the heart to look me in my face? Fuckin' pussy."

A sarcastic and patronizing laugh exploded out of Malak. "So you want to see it?"

"Yes, I wanna see it coming!" Johnnie said, cutting Malak off, before he could finish asking his question. "At least treat me like a man!"

"But you're not a man! You're a boy who hasn't even figured out how to fake it yet!" Malak chuckled to himself and considered the request again. "Treat you like a man? Ok..."

Malak carefully repositioned himself, so as not to give any leverage to Johnnie. Grabbing the boy by the back of his neck, in order to control the smaller man's movements, he pushed himself up to his feet. This motion left Malak's body bent over. He was able to keep Johnnie's body pressed against the floor.

As Malak stood up straight, he used his power and might to control and pick the helpless Johnnie up off the floor as well. But he didn't allow Johnnie to stand upright as he was. Instead, Johnnie was now bent over, in front of Malak, but facing away from him.

"Sometimes you really need to be careful of what you wish for," Malak said.

"Yeah? Why is that?" Johnnie said. He was now able to freely move the arm that had previously been pinned under him.

For Johnnie, this was a good thing. He quickly embraced his body with the freed hand by placing it under his other arm.

"Don't! Move!" Malak said. He gave Johnnie a strong shake by the neck to reinforce his point. He had also begun walking around Johnnie, so that when he finally decided to lift Johnnie's torso upright, they would be looking at each other. Face to face. Providing the dying man his last request.

Malak stood in front of Johnnie. "Well, as the cliché goes..." Malak was holding Johnnie down by a fistful of his hair. He slowly lifted him, all the while, still in control. "Be care what you wish for..."

"Because you just might get it!" Using the formerly pinned arm that was now holding his side, Johnnie dropped his hand to reveal he was holding a small hatchet. It was too late for Malak to do anything about it. Johnnie swung the tool with an upward force that split Malak's chin once it connected.

The hatchet opened Malak's chin and didn't stop until it reached the bridge of his nose.

Malak was under the impression that the huge axe, discarded earlier, was Johnnie's only weapon. But Johnnie spent his time on the floor, freeing the hatchet that was secretly hidden in its underarm holster.

The man's chin was split in two. Blood was everywhere. Stumbling backwards, in an effort to retreat, Malak tripped and landed on his back. All he could do was try to hold his face together and keep his jaw from falling out.

His pain was unbearable. He was on the floor twitching, his body was convulsing. Johnnie dropped the hatchet at Malak's feet and walked over to the axe, across the room.

"You talked about hiding in patience..." Johnnie said. He picked up the axe and walked back to Malak. "...and waiting for the moment." Johnnie heaved the huge axe above his head. "How'd I do?"

And with one swing, Malak was decapitated.

Chapter 77

"You just don't get it, Anthony. You mourn over him like he was some great guru. But Marco was more like a dime store magician."

"Really. So far, you're the only one here with tricks." I looked back at Aguilar. The magician's assistant.

"Cheap misdirection," Nick Nick said. "Marco had the entire District in fear. But it wasn't him they really were scared of. It was the work you did. And everything I did, before you.

"Fear allowed him to move through these alleys. It was fear that kept others from competing against his business. And over time, fear became confused with respect. They are not the same. You and I built what he had, through fear. He was respected because of the fear we put in this city!

"How dare he decide to shut it all down without consulting the very people who made him? Contrary to what he believed, he didn't build his business, we did!"

"You think that justifies what you've done?" I said.

"I would have loved for you to work with me on this, but I knew you wouldn't appreciate the bigger picture.

We have an opportunity to control all of it from Virginia to Maryland, and everything in between.

"This isn't personal, Anthony. It's solely about the business."

"I don't know. Sounds like you're in your feelings to me."

Nick Nick smiled at me. I could've sworn I saw the devil in his eyes. "Like I said. I knew you wouldn't appreciate the bigger picture. It was a pleasure working with you, Anthony."

Nick Nick pivoted toward the detective. "Aguilar!" He called out. "Now if you don't mind."

But before Aguilar could pull the trigger, a blaring siren and blinding red and blue lights careened through the alley entrance behind him. It couldn't have been the cops we were hearing off in the distance. These sirens weren't turned on until the car entered the alleyway.

The car was moving at full speed, past Aguilar's car, and Aguilar was in the way. The terror of being mowed down by a three thousand pound vehicle caused him to turn completely around and fire at the car moving in his direction.

Three bullets hit the windshield, but by the time he could let off another round, the car crashed into the detective. His gun flew out of his hand; he fell under the carriage. The car rolled over him.

When the car came to a complete stop, I finally got a clear view past the bullet-riddled windshield. Smitty poked his head over the dashboard and then leaned out his open window.

"As soon as he started shooting, I had to duck down!" he yelled with excitement. "Are you ok?!"

Nick Nick was frozen in astonishment. How quickly the tables had turned back in my favor. Aguilar's gun had slid in my direction and was now just a few inches from my feet.

Not wasting any time, I grabbed and aimed it at Nick Nick. "Yeah. I'm ok."

The approaching sirens weren't lost on me. They were getting louder. Probably just a few minutes away. Johnnie came tumbling through the back door. He was bloodied, but looked very much alive.

He walked over to me and said, "What are you waiting for?"

"He was probably waiting for you," Nick Nick said. "The prick wanted a bigger audience."

"Not quite." I handed the gun to Johnnie. "This go 'round, I wanna be the audience. He's all yours."

With the gun pointed squarely at Nick Nick's chest, Johnnie flashed his first genuine smile in a while. "Anything you wanna say?"

"Whatever you're going to do, boy... Just do—"

Johnnie didn't even let him finish his sentence. He put two bullets into Nick Nick's chest. The man's body twisted and spun around, finally landing the ground.

Johnnie held the gun in front of him for a few extra seconds. I grabbed it from him and began wiping it down.

"Leave it. It belongs to the cop," I said. "Now let's get out of here before the entire department shows up."

Johnnie nodded his head and walked to the car. Off at the alley's opening, we saw his sister Jena. As soon as Nick Nick fell, she was leading Coco toward the car. They had watched the whole ordeal unfold.

"Jena!" Johnnie called out. Jena left Coco and ran for her brother. He collapsed into her arms. She pulled him into the car, in order to care for his wounds, as best she could.

Coco hadn't taken another step. She was motionless. I could tell she was debating on whether it was safe to come with us.

The cop sirens sounded like they were less than sixty seconds away.

"We don't have time, Coco. You have to come with us! Right now!"

"No!" she shouted back. Her decision had been made. "I'm not coming!"

I ran to Coco and held her by both arms. "Listen. I can't tell you that the cops coming aren't Nick Nick's guys. You run the risk that they are. And if that's the case, you're dead. Do you understand? They won't let you live.

"Now get in the car. You can be mad at me later."

Without giving Coco more time to think about it, I picked her up off of the ground, cradled her in my arms, and shoved her in the back seat. She protested a little, pounding her fist, and then the door slammed shut.

I ran around to the front passenger side and hopped in. Before I could close the door, Smitty was already reversing out of the alley, at full speed, with the lights and siren on full blast. If there was any question to whether Detective Aguilar, who was still under the car, was dead, that question was now answered.

Looking through the side view mirror, I could see cop cars turn the corner and pull into the alleyway as we pulled off. If we had stayed one minute more, we would have all been on our way to jail…if we were lucky.

Epilogue

Chapter 78

It was quiet. The loudest sound in the apartment was the hum of the refrigerator. She wasn't in any condition to hold a real conversation, and I didn't feel like talking anyway. But my presence meant that I was willing to give it a try. Maybe start a new relationship.

Since Marco's death, I thought more about the importance of having a parent in my life. Marco was the surrogate. He was the father I never had. And since I purposely stayed away from my mother, he was the only person I associated with parenthood.

Coco said something to me some time ago. "*You can't blame her, you know. It's not her fault.*"

And she was right. It wasn't her fault. Even as a teen, I was advanced enough to know that someone suffering from a mental illness didn't know they were sick. I knew this, and still blamed her for everything that was said. Especially for the one thing that was done.

But this was a new day. I had made efforts in the past, but they were halfhearted. The least I could do was give a hundred percent effort at building a relationship with the only real parent that I had. After escaping death…again…it was clear that the next day wasn't promised. I needed to do all that I could to maximize the fragile present.

So I sat, staring out the living room window, while she was in what she referred to as her "favorite spot" on the couch. There was nothing outside for me see, but pretending to be interested in what was going on out there kept my mind preoccupied. And it also kept me in the room.

"Bomani came to see me the other day," she said.

Here we go, I thought. "That's unlikely, ma. Life without parole usually means life without parole."

"I'm not making this up. He sat right there." She pointed to the chair I was sitting in. "And we had a good conversation too. I told him everything, so now the both of you know. Maybe y'all can work together to help protect your mother? I don't want them coming after me again, Jelani."

"It's ok, ma. I've got you," I said. But what I really wanted to say was, *"No one ever came after you the first time."*

"Ok?" She mocked. "It's not. You know they still want me dead!"

There were no microscopic cameras embedded in the wall to monitor her actions. She ripped apart every alarm clock, radio, and phone, looking for bugging devices that didn't exist.

And that was my cue to leave. Once she starting talking about the conspiracies to have her murdered, it meant her delusions were in full swing. I had never been emotionally strong enough to sit through psychotic rants.

"It's time for me to go. I've some work I need to finish," I lied. I walked over and kissed her on the cheek.

She sensed I was rushing out and grabbed me by the hand. "I'm sorry, baby. I'm sorry." She began to cry a bit. "I didn't mean to," she stammered out.

"No, no, no. It's just I have some things I have to finish," I lied again. "I'll be back soon."

That wasn't as much of a lie. I intended on coming back, but it wouldn't be as soon as she would have liked. Trying to reconcile our relationship was harder that I thought it would be. Near death experience, or not.

"I didn't mean to," she cried out again. "You forgive me? I thought you was working with those dogs who were trying to kill me. I didn't know! You forgive me?!"

Like clockwork. Every time I got ready to leave, the melodrama was turned up another notch. I could no longer tell if it was part of her psychosis or if she was being manipulative. The easiest thing to do was always to answer her question.

"Yes, ma." I kissed her on the cheek again. "I forgive you." Another lie.

But in truth, I didn't.

All I could do was hold on to the memory of the night that I left her to stay with the Ribisi family. It was three in the morning. And there I was, bewildered and stumbling out of the house. She thought I was working for the imaginary people she believed was trying to kill her. Me. Her own son.

Try to work on our relationship? Yes. But forgive her, I couldn't. One inch to the left and I'd be dead.

How can I forgive you? You stabbed me.

Chapter 79

"I know you're looking at me!" She called through the door, before banging on it again. "Let me in, Jelani!"

I stood as still as I could, but it was no use. She was right. I was standing just on the other side of the door, looking through the peephole. She banged again.

Being completely honest, I was intrigued. The last time we spoke was that dreaded morning in the alley. Since then, she made it clear she didn't want to have anything to do with me. I left voicemail messages, without a reply. Emails went unreturned. I even stopped by her place unannounced. And she did exactly what I was doing to her now. She ignored me.

After all of that, I was done. I had lost the only father I had known. I had lost my road dog Humpty. And I also lost my best friend, who was potentially the love of my life.

So why was she here? Why now? At the moment, my curiosity outweighed my desire to be a recluse.

"Fine!" she said. "Be a hermit then!"

Coco turned to walk away. Just then, I opened the door.

"What do you want?" I said.

She turned back around. "To see if you're ok," she said with an attitude. "You can't go disappearing off the face of the earth."

"Why not? You did it."

"No, I didn't. I disappeared from you. Not the entire planet. There's a difference."

"Mmm. Good to know it was just me."

"You've got to admit, almost losing my life gives me the right to rethink our relationship."

"So, why are you here?" I said.

Coco walked over and spoke to me in a softer tone. "Jena's worried about you. Johnnie too. They've been trying to call you and they've even stopped by. You're alienating yourself and pushing people out again. So they asked me—"

"There's that therapist talk again. And what's with being best buds with the Ribisi's all of a sudden?" I interrupted.

"They *asked* me," she continued, "to check in with you and see that you hadn't hung yourself or something. It's been nearly ten weeks and you haven't spoken to anyone." I was standing in my doorway when Coco walked over to me. As a result, she was able to take a peek in my apartment as she spoke. "Oh my God! Your place is a mess!" she shouted, pushing past me. The softness was gone.

Now fully in the apartment, she ran throughout the rooms and made a quick assessment of my situation. "When was the last time you cleaned this place? Never mind. Don't answer that. This is not you, Jelani!"

"I'll be fine," I said. Coco looked at me incredulously. I knew what that look meant.

"Ok. I want to you to clean this place. Tonight. I'll be back tomorrow."

"You're coming back?"

"That's what I said! And I'll keep coming back, but you've got to work on being your old self. Because this…" She pointed to the mess around my apartment. "...is not a good look for you."

The thought of seeing Coco again had me feeling better immediately. "Maybe we'll be able to get something to eat…or something?" I asked, hoping I wasn't pressing my luck.

"We'll see." She walked out the door. "I'll see you tomorrow, Jelani. And maybe the next time someone other than me stops by or calls, you'll be a little more engaging. Give it a try."

Leaning against the doorframe, I stared as she walked away. I whispered to myself, "We'll see."

I shut the door and was still on a Coco-high. *I have a lot of work to do,* I thought to myself. I rummaged through the hallway closet for a minute and pulled out my vacuum cleaner.

"She wants clean, she'll get clean."

I plugged in the machine and got ready to let her roar, when my cell phone rang. I was sure it was Coco, because she had just left. It made sense to me.

"Hey hun," I said when I picked up the phone. "I'll be free this weekend too, if you want me to be!" Halfway joking. Halfway for real.

"Hey Anthony," the voice on the other line said. And I knew who it was immediately. But she sounded distressed, which worried me.

"Jena. Are you ok?"

"Yeah. I'm fine," she said. "You've been M.I.A. for a while. And I've been trying to reach you.'

"I know. I'm just starting to pull out of my funk. I'll be around more often."

"Good. I'm glad to hear that. I'll need you around," she said. "—because Anthony, I'm pregnant."

And that's when I dropped my phone.

THE END

20525766R00174

Made in the USA
Middletown, DE
29 May 2015